TIRAMISU OR MURDER

AN ITALIAN-AMERICAN COZY MYSTERY SERIES
BOOK 5

M.P. BLACK

My love — this is for everything, always.

1

"I can't leave Moroni's," I said. "The bakery is like a second home to me."

Nat grabbed the branch of a tree and hauled himself up the ridge we were climbing. "Well, what would Eve Silver do?"

"It's not that simple," I said.

"You know what Eve would say?"

I sighed. "Yes, I know."

Nat said it anyway, quoting Eve Silver: "*The solution is always simpler than you think.*" Then he paused, looking thoughtful. He flipped his floppy fair hair out of his face and adjusted his glasses. "Of course, season three was full of overcomplicated plots, and you and Adam Gold rarely found a simple solution."

He was referring to the character I used to play on America's most popular detective show, *Silver & Gold*. Back in my previous life. Before witness protection. Before coming to Carmine and becoming Bernie Smyth.

I put a hand on the tree Nat had used to pull himself up,

and I paused. I drew in a deep breath, savoring the cool, fresh air of the Carmine Woods.

Nat reached the top of the ridge. I trudged up the steep terrain, struggling over rocks and broken branches. Soon, I stood by Nat's side.

Far off to our left rose the Overlook. And straight ahead, through miles of dense trees, I saw hints of water. Lake Carmine. We'd come deep into the woods on this hike.

"Wow, look at this view," I said.

Nat nudged me. "Don't change the subject."

Soon after U.S. Marshall Roberta La Rosa provided me with a new identity as Bernie Smyth in Carmine, New Jersey, Nat Natale had become my best friend. As a long-time fan of *Silver & Gold*, he'd also guessed my true identity: Bernadette Kovac, the actress who played Eve Silver, and who testified against Jay Casanova in his gun-and-drug trafficking trial. And he knew me well enough to know when I was deflecting or dawdling.

We started walking along the ridge. A rough track, either made by people or animals, ran along the rugged ground.

I sighed. "All right, if the solution is so simple, what would Eve Silver do?"

"Before I answer that," he said, vaulting over a fallen tree that blocked our path, "tell me, how does Angelica feel about you leaving the bakery?"

"She's supportive, of course. You know Angelica. She's always supportive."

Angelica Moroni, owner of Moroni's Italian Bakery, wasn't just my boss. She was like family to me.

I climbed over the tree, too. But less gracefully, straddling it first and then sliding down the other side. Then Nat and I followed the track as it wound down the sloping ridge toward a gully.

"Good," Nat said. "Now, what does Chief Tedesco say? I imagine our chief of police has an opinion."

"She's supportive, too," I said. "In fact, she's offered to provide me with an internship. It's not totally kosher, but she says she's going to bend the rules so I can join the force as a 'consultant.'"

"So Angelica's happy to set you free, and Chief Tedesco will help you get the formal experience you need. Then, after a few months of working with the Carmine Police Department, you can apply to detective school and become a professional investigator. See, it is simple."

We reached the bottom of the gully and clambered over slippery rocks. The passage narrowed between our ridge on the left and another rising steeply to the right. Nat, the more experienced hiker, took the lead.

"It's not called 'detective school,'" I said, "and, for the record, you need years—not months—of experience to become a certified professional investigator. Besides, I'm having second thoughts."

Nat laughed. "You always have second thoughts. But just wait, the next time there's a crime to be solved in Carmine, you won't be hemming and hawing. You'll jump right in."

"I don't know, Nat. This is different. This is about changing my entire life."

The gully twisted. As we came around a corner, Nat stopped. I was still catching up.

"I love my life in Carmine," I explained, balancing on a big rock and stepping over to the long flat one Nat stood on.

He wasn't moving. Just standing there, staring straight ahead.

I said, "There's a part of me that doesn't want to rock the boat. Part of me is afraid to choose between Moroni's and detective work. I mean, bakery assistant might not be the perfect job for me. But what if I try my hand at being a private investigator and discover I miss the—"

I looked up and froze.

"—mark," I finished, as I saw what Nat was staring at.

A man sat on the ground, his back to a tree. A hunter. He wore a shirt and pants with a camouflage pattern and a green vest with plenty of pockets. A rifle lay among the leaves by his boots.

But it wasn't the hunting gear that stood out.

It was the arrow buried in his chest. The blood blooming on his shirt. His empty, open eyes.

Nat gaped at the dead man. I grabbed my phone, all other thoughts vanishing from my mind.

"Chief Tedesco," I said when she answered my call, "we've found a body."

2

Nat and I sat in the two chairs in front of Officer Fontana's desk at the Carmine Police Department headquarters. Fontana was typing up our statements on his computer while listening to the radio.

"Where's Chief Tedesco?" I asked.

"At the scene of the crime," Fontana said, distracted, his eyes still on his screen. "You know, with the county coroner and forensics."

"I thought—" I cut myself off. And gave Nat a puzzled look. He shrugged, as if to say he was just as surprised.

Nat and I had waited about 20 minutes for Officers Fontana and Ferrante to locate us in the woods. Then they secured the area with tape. I expected to wait around until Chief Tedesco turned up, and then join her as she kicked off the investigation. After all, wasn't that the idea—that I was going to assist her?

Instead, Fontana escorted us back to HQ to question us about our discovery. Like two ordinary citizens.

"Any idea when she'll be back?" I asked.

"Pretty soon, I guess," Fontana said. "Although with the OPS agent around, things are taking longer."

"The OPS agent? Who's that?"

"Shh..." he hushed me. "I wanna hear this."

The DJ on the radio announced the daily music quiz, and Fontana leaned back in his chair. Apparently, the quiz was a bigger deal than typing up our statements. A smile quirked his lips and his eyebrows knitted into a concentrated frown.

"*Now, which of the three songs I just played are officially intergalactic? Call this number if you know the answer...*"

Fontana let out a huff of frustration. "Officially intergalactic? *Madone!* What's that supposed to mean?"

"What songs did he play?" Nat asked.

"Louis Prima's 'Just a Gigolo,'" Fontana said. "Sam Cooke's 'Cupid.' And Chuck Berry's 'Johnny B. Goode.' It's gotta be Louis Prima, right? I mean, Sam Cooke and Chuck Berry are great and all, but Louis Prima..."

He gestured with his hands—both of them palms up as if weighing something—while pursing his lips, one of the million ways Italians communicated without using words.

"It's gotta be Louis Prima."

"It's 'Johnny B. Goode,'" Nat said.

Fontana gave Nat a suspicious look. "You sound pretty confident. You sure?"

"I'm sure. In 1977, we sent the two Voyagers into deep space. Each carried a Golden Record with a bunch of music and sounds. One of them was 'Johnny B. Goode.'" Nat grinned. "Imagine that somewhere in a galaxy far, far away, aliens are boogying to Chuck Berry."

Fontana glanced at me, his look still skeptical.

"You can bet Nat is right," I said. "He's a history buff.

And a total geek. Why do you think he works at our historical society?"

"Guilty," Nat said.

That seemed to convince Fontana, and he grabbed his cell phone, got out of his swivel chair, and walked away. In the distance, I heard him excitedly state his name and number, and then say, "'Johnny B. Goode'—the answer is 'Johnny B. Goode.'"

Meanwhile, I was turning around and craning my neck, hoping to catch sight of Chief Tedesco. I checked the time. We'd been at the Carmine PD for over an hour. Where was she?

3

When Chief Tedesco strode into the Carmine Police Department, a man followed closely behind her. He wore a dark blue suit with a laminated ID pinned to his chest. At a distance, all I could read were the large, bold letters "OPS." He held a clipboard against his side.

"Miss Smyth," Chief Tedesco said when she saw me. "Please follow me."

Miss Smyth!? The last time she called me that was back when we first met each other, and she'd accused me of murder. A bad start. But we'd left that behind us—far behind us—and I considered Chief Diana Tedesco not only a great cop, but also a great friend. So what the heck was going on?

As I stood, Nat got up to join me. But Chief Tedesco waved a hand.

"Not you, Mr. Natale. I'll interview the two of you separately." She leveled her gaze at Officer Fontana, giving him a stern look. "As per our procedures."

Officer Fontana looked confused. "But Chief, it's just Bernie and Nat…"

Chief Tedesco winced and glanced at the OPS guy, who gave a slight nod and noted something on his clipboard.

"Come along, Miss Smyth," Chief Tedesco said.

I followed her into an interrogation room. A pitcher of water and a paper cup stood on the table. She indicated that I should sit down. I did.

The OPS guy leaned against a nearby wall. As if he was staying out of the way, while still remaining in view. Chief Tedesco pulled out the chair across from me and sat down.

She looked me in the eye. As if she wanted to tell me something. She motioned with her eyes toward the guy to her right, and I understood: all this was for his benefit.

"Agent Mabley from the newly established OPS field operations is joining us today," Chief Tedesco said, sounding oddly formal. "He's here to assess my performance, and so you should feel free to speak to me as you would normally."

I glanced over at the guy, and he gave a nod. No smile. He gazed at me with a coldness that made me think I was just another item to be ticked off on his clipboard.

He said, "Eric Mabley, Office of Professional Standards, New Jersey State Police. As Chief Tedesco alluded to, I'm conducting a field audit of the Carmine Police Department." Then he nodded at Chief Tedesco. "You may proceed."

Something flicked across Chief Tedesco's face. Only for an instant. But I knew her well enough to recognize the emotion: anger. Who was Agent Mobley to tell her that she was allowed to proceed in her own police department? But apparently, he did have some authority over her, because she obviously suppressed her feelings and launched into a series of questions about what Nat and I had been doing in the woods, how we'd found the body, and what—if anything —we'd disturbed at the scene of the crime.

The same questions Officer Fontana had asked. But it made sense that Chief Tedesco would want me to repeat my story. Only, under normal circumstances, we would've done it over coffee and cannoli at Moroni's.

I answered the questions. Occasionally, Agent Mobley wrote something, his pen scratching on the paper. It made Chief Tedesco grit her teeth. I'd rarely seen her so on edge.

"That concludes our questioning for now. Thank you, Miss Smyth. You're free to go now."

Chief Tedesco got up. I did, too.

As we were filing out of the interrogation room, she held open the door for Agent Mobley.

"Please," she said. "After you, Agent Mobley. And go ahead, Miss Smyth."

Agent Mobley left the room, and I followed him, but as I was passing Chief Tedesco by the door, she grabbed my arm. She dropped her voice to a murmur.

"I promised you could be my assistant." She shook her head. "I'm sorry, Bernie. The OPS is breathing down my neck. And now, with their new field operations, it's not just a bunch of white-collar stiffs auditing police departments— they're sending so-called 'agents' out to watch our every move."

My heart sank. I could say goodbye to the internship at the Carmine PD. I'd been counting on that to get me the formal law enforcement experience I needed to apply for a private investigator license. Now what was I going to do?

"I understand," I mumbled.

"Understand what?" Agent Mobley asked, suddenly materializing by the doorway. He held his clipboard ready, as if he wanted to record my every word.

"I understand," I said, "it's time for me to go home."

4

When I shuffled into Moroni's, my hands thrust deep into my pockets, disappointment sat on my shoulders like a ton of bricks. My plans had fallen apart. I was stuck.

But then the familiar fragrance of our Italian bakery—a sweet, baked heavenliness—washed over me. I breathed it in. It smelled like home. I looked around.

Moroni's looked as delightful as ever. The red-checkered curtains. The walls of the cafe decorated with prints of Italian scenery. The long glass counter filled with mounds of cookies and cakes.

A few customers sat at tables, drinking cappuccinos and americanos and nibbling on pignoli cookies and cannolis. Overhead, the speakers played a song by Dean Martin.

If my plans to become a private investigator had to be put on hold, this wasn't the worst place to be stuck, was it? Maybe the universe was telling me something. Maybe this was my chance to double down on my work for Angelica— and prove I could be the best bakery assistant she could imagine.

When I first came to town, Angelica had offered me a job at Moroni's. But it was more than a job. It was an invitation into a family. Now, I couldn't imagine a life without Angelica, her brother, Carlo, and all the other wonderful people in Carmine.

Angelica emerged from the back—the door leading to the bakery and the office—and she was carrying a big tray of rainbow cookies.

When she saw me, her face lit up with a smile. "Bernie! Let me arrange these cookies, and then I want to hear all about your new investigation."

I shouldn't have been surprised that Angelica already knew about the dead man in the woods—gossip traveled fast in our little town.

Angelica arranged the rainbow cookies in the glass counter.

"Let me help," I said, and I headed behind the counter. I reached for the apron I usually wore. But the peg was empty.

"Angelica," I said. "Do you know where my apron is?"

Angelica smiled, straightening up from her task. "You're not the only one with good news."

"Uh, what good news?"

"Well, since you'll be working full time with Chief Tedesco, I decided I'd better get some extra help."

A little worm squirmed in my gut. "Extra help?"

At that moment, Lily came out of the bakery in the back. Lily worshipped Angelica, seeing her as a role model for her own baking ambitions. She fit right into Moroni's, despite her edgy appearance: She sported a shaved head, a row of earrings lining one lobe, and purple lipstick. Under her apron, she wore a death metal t-shirt.

No, not under her apron. Under my apron.

When she saw me, she broke into a big smile. "Hey, Bernie."

Angelica put an arm around Lily's shoulders. "Lily graduated from high school, and she's applied to an undergraduate program at a culinary institute in the city."

"I want to be a pastry chef," Lily said, beaming. "But first I'm taking a year off to earn some money. College is expensive."

"And that's why she'll be working at Moroni's," Angelica said. Her smile widened. "After all, you won't have time to help, Bernie. So it's perfect. Don't you think?"

That little worm in my stomach had grown big, and it tightened into a painful knot.

"Yeah," I muttered. "Perfect."

Lily got busy arranging the rest of the rainbow cookies. A customer came through the door—the little bell jingling—and asked for a box of cannolis. Angelica served him.

Meanwhile, I drifted away from the counter, my hands dug into my pockets again. I collapsed onto a chair at an empty table.

I felt sick to my stomach. Chief Tedesco couldn't include me in her investigation. Angelica didn't need me anymore. So, what was I going to do?

Behind me, I heard a phone ringing. Angelica answered with an enthusiastic, "Hi, Nat!"

Nat. Maybe he could help me get a job at the public library where he worked for the Carmine historical society. At least until I could figure out what I was going to do with my life. But I had no qualifications to work at the public library. Unless they needed ex-actresses who had a knack for investigating crime.

I sighed. Who was I kidding? I wasn't going to get a job at the library.

Angelica appeared by my side. She put a hand on my shoulder.

"*Cara mia*, why didn't you tell me? Nat called and explained everything about Chief Tedesco, and how she's excluded you from the investigation."

I shrugged. "There's nothing I can do about it."

"But there is something *I* can do about it," Angelica said firmly. She undid her apron and pulled it off. "Come on. Lily can manage Moroni's for a while. You and me, we're going to see Cosimo."

I stared at her, surprised. "Who's Cosimo?"

"He's my cousin," Angelica said. "And he's going to give you a job."

5

On the fourth floor of a derelict office building in a run-down neighborhood in Newark, Angelica and I stopped in front of a door with a small brass sign. One screw had come loose and the sign dangled. I turned my head to read it.

"*Cosimo Investigations.*" I glanced at Angelica. "Your cousin is a private investigator? Why didn't you tell me on the ride over? And why have you never mentioned him before?"

Angelica gave me a weak smile. "I never thought we'd need his help. But things are—"

"Desperate?"

"I didn't say that."

But she sure looked like she meant it. She turned away from me and rang the bell. No sound. So she knocked on the door. A muffled shout from within told us to "come in."

We stepped right into a small office that reeked of cigar smoke. An old wooden desk dominated the space, and behind it sat a small, rotund man in a white shirt and suspenders. His belly pressed against his suspenders. A splatter of something red—maybe sauce—stained his shirt. He chewed on a short, wet stub of cigar as he cradled an old phone under his ear.

"Yeah, yeah, you'll get the photos tomorrow."

He slammed the phone down on its cradle. His unibrow shot up when he saw us, then bent into a frown.

"Angelica," he rasped. "You in some kind of trouble?"

"Hi, Cosimo. Good to see you."

Cosimo waved a pudgy hand, dismissing the greeting.

"What is it? Tax evasion? Did a customer claim to choke on a cookie, and now they're suing?"

The phone rang. He picked it up and told the person to please hold. Then opened a drawer, pressed something inside, which set off a recording of smooth jazz. He dropped the phone inside the drawer and closed it, muffling the music. The wire trailed down over the edge of the desk.

I stared. I'd never seen a system for on-hold music like that.

Cosimo rolled the cigar stump in his mouth. "You know cousin Ralph's in jail?"

"No." Angelica shook her head. "Again?"

"Oh, yes. Counterfeit goods." He sighed. "Again."

They launched into a conversation about a whole range of first and second cousins I'd never heard of. A disproportionate amount of them seemed to be in trouble with the law.

During the conversation with Angelica, Cosimo opened the drawer, turned off the music, and fished out the phone. He spoke in raspy, rapid-fire sentences, once again putting off a client "until tomorrow." Then hung up and went back to talking to Angelica about their cousins.

The phone rang again.

Meanwhile, I looked around.

Old metal filing cabinets lined the walls with stacks of manila folders and loose papers on top. Cardboard boxes stood pressed into a corner, a couple of them with their flaps open, revealing more folders and papers. Bookshelves were crammed with books, some lined up, others on the edges, teetering in chaotic piles.

In between the books—and the stacks of paperwork on the filing cabinets—sat an odd assortment of knickknacks: a plastic Statue of Liberty, a Virgin Mary snow globe, a bowl full of colored glass beads. But also this: an antique glass bottle marked "arsenic," a single bullet casing, and, inside an empty jam jar, what looked disconcertingly like a prosthetic eye.

I moved around the room, looking at more oddities: a stuffed lizard mounted on a log, a disc made out of gold (or something resembling gold) with strange markings on it, and a framed text written in an unfamiliar geometric script.

I smelled Cosimo before I saw him by my side. A mix of cigar and fried food. He said, "It's written in Utopian. It's a murderer's confession. He killed a rival academic at a science fiction conference, and the *stunad* thought it would be cute to leave clues in a made-up language." His tone shifted. So did the cigar in this mouth. "Angelica tells me you need my help."

"I do?"

His unibrow collapsed over his bulbous nose.

"Oh," I said. "Yes, I do."

I looked over at Angelica for help. She stepped over to us.

"Actually, I think Bernie can help you, Cosimo. I think you can help each other. You're a busy man..."

Cosimo nodded.

"…and you're far from our part of Jersey, where I bet you get some cases now and then."

"Got one right now in Carmine," he said. "But what's your point, Angelica? Get to it."

Angelica smiled her sweet smile. Like it was made of confectioners' sugar.

"Cousin," she said, and placed a hand on his shoulder. "How would you like an assistant to help you with cases in the Carmine area? Bernie could help."

Cosimo shook his head. "Fugeddaboudit. I don't work with no one. Never have, never will."

At some point, the phone had stopped ringing. Now it started again.

"You're swamped, Cosimo," Angelica said, gesturing toward the phone. "That thing never stops ringing. Even just offloading one case to an assistant might make a difference. Didn't you say you have a case in Carmine?"

Cosimo stared at Angelica. The phone rang and rang and rang. Then, with a low grumble, he returned to his desk and picked up the phone.

"Cosimo Investigations," he barked. Then his voice softened a little. "Yes, Mrs. Romano. Yes, I did say I would drop by last week. How about—" He flipped through a planner on his desk. But the person on the line apparently beat him to it. "Well, I don't know about getting to Carmine tomorrow. I got a court appearance at 11 am and then a guy I'm tailing in the afternoon, so…"

Angelica nudged me. She gave me a pointed look. Obviously telling me this was my chance to step in.

Her plan, as I understood it, was simple: If Chief Tedesco couldn't provide me with the experience I needed to become a private investigator, then her cousin Cosimo could. Judging by the constantly ringing phone and the chaos in his office, Cosimo needed help. It wouldn't be like working alongside Chief Tedesco, that was for sure. But what other options did I have right now?

I stepped over to the desk and whispered, "Cosimo, you don't need to go to Carmine. I can go see Mrs. Romano tomorrow. I'll report back to you."

Cosimo, still listening to the voice on the phone, gave me a skeptical look. Then said, "Mrs. Romano, my apologies, but please hold."

For a second I thought he'd drop the phone into the drawer again. But instead he placed a hand over the phone's mouthpiece and said to me, "You even know the first thing about investigating?"

"I know—"

"Yeah, yeah, the Eve Silver thing. I never liked the show. Give me *Columbo* or *The Rockford Files* any day of the week. But what I'm talking about is Cosimo's Number One Rule."

"What's Cosimo's Number One Rule?"

"See," he said, throwing a hand into the air, exasperated. "You don't even know."

"What I don't know, I can learn."

He considered me for a moment. "Cosimo's Number One Rule is this: *It's the client's way or it's the highway.* That's the rule. Now and then, a client will say, 'You know best, Cosimo. Go ahead and run the show.' But it's rare. Most clients have a good idea of what they want: 'Cosimo, my wife's cheating on me and I want proof.' Never mind if there's a way to save the marriage. The guy wants photos of his wife."

"But what if the wife isn't cheating on him?" I suggested.

"Then you still give the client what he wants. Photos of his wife. At the mall. At the tennis club. A whole week's worth. Then, if the client wants another week, you've got a steady gig, until the *mamaluke* realizes his wife isn't cheating on him." He rolled his cigar from one corner of his mouth to the other. "You got it?"

"I got it."

He stared at me. The unibrow low on his forehead. "Don't make me regret this."

"I won't. I promise."

He uncovered the phone and put it back to his ear.

"Mrs. Romano," he rasped. "You're in luck. My assistant's available. She'll pay you a visit tomorrow morning."

6

"Cosimo?" Chief Tedesco blurted. "What were you thinking?"

"What's wrong with Cosimo?" Nat asked.

"Have you met the guy?"

Chief Tedesco shook her head.

Carlo, Angelica's brother and owner of Carlo's Restaurant, stood by our table. He folded his arms across his chest.

"Careful what you say about my cousin."

Angelica, Nat, and I had been eating dinner at Carlo's when Chief Tedesco joined us. I sat next to Nat. Across from us sat Angelica and Chief Tedesco.

A soundtrack of gentle jazz played in the background. The carpeted floors, heavy drapes, even acoustic paneling in the ceiling muted every sound to a soft hush.

Well, almost every sound.

Carlo said, "Cosimo solved the famous Bianchi kidnapping case."

"That was 20 years ago," Chief Tedesco said.

"He's famous among us Italians."

"He's infamous."

Maria, Carlo's waitress, came out of the back carrying a tray heaped with food. Our dinner. She set down plates with antipasto: a caprese salad with fresh mozzarella and tomatoes and basil leaves drizzled with olive oil and balsamic, grilled fennel, a dish full of pesto, a taleggio cheese, prosciutto ham, and a bowl of olives. And, of course, a basket full of freshly baked bread.

"You talking about Cosimo?" she said as she laid out the food. "He helped my Uncle Lorenzo prove his third wife had been cheating on him all along, so he could get his marriage annulled before he died." She swiftly made the sign of the cross. "It meant he could rest in peace."

"And it meant his kids," Chief Tedesco added, "who paid Cosimo's fees, inherited everything."

Maria shrugged. "Better them than that—"

"My point is," Chief Tedesco continued, speaking over the litany of Italian curse words Maria used to describe Uncle Lorenzo's third ex-wife, "that Cosimo's more interested in making money than getting to the truth."

"But it's not like I have any other options," I said.

Chief Tedesco winced. "And I'm sorry about that. I couldn't honor my promise to you. But with the OPS breathing down my neck..."

"You don't have to apologize," I said. "I understand."

"I barely managed to shake Agent Mabley tonight—he even wants to follow me around after hours."

"Chief," I said, reaching across the table and touching her hand. "I understand."

She took my hand and squeezed it. "I'm sorry this has forced you to go to someone like Cosimo."

I dipped a piece of bread in the pesto and stuffed it in

my mouth, savoring the rich flavor. I wished we could talk about the food instead of focusing on my new boss's shortcomings. Which I didn't feel great about.

"What's the big deal?" Nat said, jumping into the conversation as he cut into a soft slice of mozzarella. "Cosimo's a professional private investigator. Which is exactly what Bernie wants to be. So working as his assistant to get experience sounds ideal."

"Well, hardly *ideal*," Chief Tedesco said.

"Oh, don't be so picky," Nat said. "Sometimes, if we want to do the things we love, we need to do stuff that isn't perfect along the way. If we wait around for perfect, we might never change our lives. And you know what that does to people."

Carlo stroked his goatee, nodding. "It kills you, slowly. You've got to pursue your dreams."

"Right," Nat said. "And isn't Cosimo, in his own way, living his dream? Even if it reeks of cigar, it's still his dream."

Chief Tedesco shrugged. "If you say so."

Nat grinned. "I say so."

"And I say we need some wine," I added, changing the subject.

I popped an olive into my mouth. Carlo headed off to get a bottle of chianti. And while we all got busy eating, I considered Nat's unusually wise words.

He was right, of course. Any misgivings I had about Cosimo were neither here nor there. The point was that, with Angelica's help, I had a chance to get real experience as an investigator. I had a chance to pursue my dream.

Carlo returned and poured the wine.

I raised my glass.

"To following our dreams," I said.

Angelica smiled. "And to Cosimo's Assistant Investigator."

I couldn't keep from grinning. It was finally happening. Tomorrow, I was going to work my first official case as an investigator.

"You won't regret it," I whispered to myself. Or maybe it was to Cosimo.

U.S. and Italian flags fluttered over Romano Auto Sales the next morning when I arrived. A variety of cars, ranging from brand new to lightly used, stood in the lot. Inside, the carpeted floors led me to a reception desk. A woman so young she barely looked out of high school gave me a big gap-toothed smile.

"Looking for a car? I'll get one of the boys to help you."

"I'm here to see Mrs. Romano. I have an appointment."

Turning to a computer screen, she tapped on her keyboard and clicked her mouse.

"Cosimo?"

"Cosimo's assistant, Bernie."

She led me down a corridor beyond the reception desk. Four offices, two on either side, with a fifth door at the very end.

In the first office to the left, a tall, gaunt man with hair that matched his dark suit was standing by the window talking on the phone. The sign outside his door said, "Joseph Romano Jr."

Across the hallway, the sign said, "Enzo Romano." The

man inside—slicked back hair, shirt open to expose chest hair and a gold necklace—also spoke on the phone. But he perched at end of his desk and, as the receptionist and I passed, he gave me a flirtatious wink.

An empty office to the left, and then across from that the sign outside said, "Michael Romano." A young, skinny guy with a pasty complexion slumped over a desk. I slowed a little. He was bent over a sketchbook, apparently drawing. Next to it lay a comic book.

Suddenly, he looked up with a jerk of the head, startled to see me. Deep rings under his eyes. He shoved the sketchbook and comic onto his lap, hiding them.

"Uh," he said, as he fiddled nervously with his pen. "Can I help you?"

The receptionist answered before I could: "She's meeting your mom, Mikey."

"Oh, all right..." he said, sounding relieved.

The receptionist escorted me through the open door at the end of the corridor.

Mrs. Romano sat behind a wide mahogany desk. She wore a pearl necklace, and although her proportions strained her business suit a little, her outfit obviously cost money.

"Sit," she ordered. Then looked at the receptionist. "Janice."

"Jenna."

"Get us some coffee. And close the door behind you."

I sat down in one of the two chairs facing her.

"So," Mrs. Romano said. "You're the assistant."

She eyed me with infinite skepticism. Once, when I was a kid, I'd been sent to the principal's office for sneaking into the teachers' lounge and finding the schedule for upcoming pop quizzes. This was the look she gave me. Heat flushed my face. I felt an irrational sense of having broken one of Mrs. Romano's rules.

"My daughter-in-law is missing," she said suddenly. "I want you to find her."

I nodded. I took out a pen and a notepad, several pages of which were already filled. Cosimo had told me everything he knew about the case. And I'd supplemented by searching online and finding a photo of Adriana.

"Adriana Romano," I said, reading from my notes. "Maiden name Giovannucci. Married to Michael Romano."

"Mikey," Mrs. Romano corrected me. "No one except for Father Bruno calls him Michael."

"Mikey" I noted in the margins of the page.

"Any idea why Adriana would—"

"Mikey is upset," Mrs. Romano cut me off. "That's why I want you to find her. Otherwise that silly girl can run off to Timbuktu for all I care. But Mikey is distraught. We're a family business, and this whole moping thing is hurting his ability to do his work."

"Which is?"

"We sell cars. If you are a real detective, you can figure that much out by yourself, can't you?" She frowned. "Don't tell me Cosimo sent a temp. We got a temp to replace Adriana at the front desk, and I'm telling you, kids nowadays have no common sense. They know the social medias, like that Tic-Tac-Toe, or whatever it's called, but they have no head for business."

Just then Jenna, the receptionist, came into the office bearing a tray with coffee, cream, and sugar.

As soon as she'd set down the coffee, Mrs. Romano waved her away.

"So Adriana was your receptionist?" I asked.

"Didn't I just say that?" Mrs. Romano let out a huff of

frustration. "Yes, she had some useless degree from university. Art and Design, I think. And so, for Mikey's sake, I did her a favor and gave her a job."

Judging by Mrs. Romano's disdain, I wondered how much Adriana felt it was a favor.

"When did Adriana leave?" I asked.

"Nine days ago."

I looked up from my notes, stunned. "Nine days? Did you talk to the police?"

"Of course. But since Adriana packed her bags and left our home by choice, Chief Tedesco tells me she can hardly be counted as a missing person."

"She left your home?"

"Yes, our home. The boys and I live at the family home on Cedar Hill."

I made a mental note of that: Adriana and her husband had lived at home with "Mom." Wouldn't that be reason enough to leave?

Mrs. Romano carried on: "And since she didn't take Mikey's car—she didn't take any of the family cars—we can't report her for theft, either. She's likely hiding somewhere."

"Why would she be hiding?"

"How should I know?" she snapped. "It's your job to find out."

"I'd like to talk to her husband, Mikey."

"No," Mrs. Romano said. "You won't bother Mikey. All you need to do is go see Adriana's good-for-nothing sister and brother. Linda and Leo Giovannucci."

"But Mikey might know—"

"Believe me, the Giovannuccis are behind all this. No doubt they're planning to squeeze money out of us Romanos."

"How would they do that?"

"They're Giovannuccis. They always find a way."

"Still, it would be helpful if I could talk to Mikey. Maybe he—"

"What part of 'no' don't you understand? Do I need to discuss your lack of professionalism with Cosimo?" She put a hand on the phone on her desk.

I could already imagine what Cosimo would say. He'd repeat Cosimo's Number One Rule: *It's the client's way or it's the highway.* I couldn't let him down on the first day of my new job.

I sighed. "No need to call Cosimo. I understand. I'll go see the Giovannuccis."

Mrs. Romano dismissed me.

8

Unfortunately, the Happy Hunter, where Linda Giovannucci worked, lay on the opposite side of town from Romano Auto Sales. And since I didn't own a car, only my canary-yellow racing bike, I worked up a sweat before rolling into the parking lot.

As I parked my bicycle by a chain-link fence and locked it, I thought of Nat. He often teased me about relying on a bike, but what more did I need? It was a quick ride from my home on Lampedusa Lane to the Moroni's. But now that I was an assistant investigator, I could see that two wheels and a pair of pedals might not be enough.

I ran my sleeve across my face, wiping off the sweat. Then strode into the hunting store.

I wandered through aisles with thermoses, tents, and racks of camouflage clothes. On the walls hung taxidermy—the stuffed heads of deer and bear and moose—as well as bows and crossbows and hunting rifles.

A glass counter near the back displayed riflescopes. A woman behind the counter in a Happy Hunter polo shirt gave me a hard smile as I approached. She wore an abundance of dark make-up, which made her look severe. The long claw-like fake nails didn't help, either. And she'd tied her dyed blonde hair into a tight ponytail. Her name tag said, "Linda."

"Can I help you?"

I hesitated. Should I tell her who I was? Or pretend to be a customer?

Her smile vanished. She narrowed her eyes. Flinty gray eyes. "I know you. You're that actress who came to Carmine and stuck your nose in everyone's business, like you friggin' own our town. Well, ya don't."

I could see my chances of acting innocent had vanished, so I decided to pull the professional card.

"I'm working for Cosimo Investigations." I flipped open my wallet, showing the laminated business card Cosimo had given me. And, since anyone could make a card like that at Staples, I flipped it shut again before Linda took a close look at it. "I'm looking into your sister's disappearance."

"Ha," Linda barked. "You're working for that witch, Mrs. Romano, aren't you? Jenna goes to my nail salon and she told me the old hag had hired a detective." She crossed her arms. "If you think I'm gonna rat out my own sister, you can fugeddaboudit."

"Mikey, Adriana's husband, is upset that she's gone."

Linda snorted. "Doesn't take much to upset that crybaby. Don't know what Adriana ever saw in him."

"Any idea where she went?"

"Anywhere but that house on Cedar Hill. I'm surprised she didn't escape that Alcatraz before. I mean, can you imagine living with a household full of Romanos?"

"Adriana left the Romanos without taking a car. Any idea if a friend picked her up?"

Linda shrugged and looked away, suddenly interested in

adjusting a stack of flyers on the counter. "She didn't have a lot of close friends. She probably took a taxi. She probably flew to California or Florida." She glanced back at me. "Yeah, that's it. She's sitting on a beach somewhere drinking friggin' piña coladas and counting her blessings she's left her *stuppiad* husband."

"Did she contact you or your brother?"

"Why would she contact me and Leo?" Again, she got busy tidying the counter. "We were never good enough for that little artsy-fartsy princess. If she reached out to anyone it was to Bud."

"Bud?"

"My other brother. Mr. Weirdo. No one's seen him for years. Not since he was discharged from the military and went off the grid. But Adriana once told me she knew how to contact him."

"Does he live in Carmine?"

She shook her head. "Told you. No one's seen him for years. He's probably living in a cabin in Alaska or out in the Rockies somewhere. You know what—" She snapped her long-nailed fingers. "—I bet that's where she is. She took a taxi to the airport and flew to see Bud in Alaska."

"So not the beach in Florida?"

Linda smiled. Crocodiles had nicer smiles. "Nah. I hope she's freezing her butt off in the middle of nowhere. She made her bed when she married an Romano. Now let her lie in it. You know what I say?"

She waited a beat for me to react to this obviously rhetorical question.

"No, what?"

"I say, good riddance."

9

If Adriana had taken a taxi, as Linda suggested, then there was one person in Carmine who would know about it. That evening, I found Primo Leone, owner of Carmine's only taxi company, at the Old Mill.

The Old Mill was Carmine's best—and only—bar. Located on the road to the woods, it was housed in the old saw mill that once fueled the town's economy. Over half a century ago. Now its exposed beams, long wooden floorboards, and rustic feel gave it a roadhouse vibe, even when the jukebox was playing Frank Sinatra, as it was when I walked in that evening.

Primo was sitting at the bar, talking to Jerry, the bartender. Or rather, Primo was talking. Jerry, who rarely spoke, was nodding as he cleaned a pint glass with a cloth. His flannel shirt and beard contrasted with Primo's old school outfit: white button-down shirt, black dress pants, and leather shoes.

I slipped onto the barstool next to Primo's and told him about my errand.

"Adriana Romano?" He shook his head. "Can't say I

remember giving her a ride recently. But Bernie, be careful —" He gave me a grandfatherly look of concern. "—these Romanos and Giovannuccis have been at each other's throats for years. You don't wanna get caught in the middle."

"Yeah, I can tell there's not a lot of love between them."

"They're like those families from Romeo and Juliet," he said. "The Montagues and Capulets."

"You read Shakespeare, Primo?"

He shook his head. "But I know a thing or two about families fighting each other."

This was true. Primo used to be a driver for the mafia before he left "the family" and retired to a quieter life as a small-town cab driver.

Primo said, "Only a week or so ago, there was a fight here at the Old Mill. Right, Jerry?" Jerry nodded, and Primo carried on: "The Romano boys were having drinks. Mikey, Enzo, and Joe. Adriana was with them. But then something happened—a disagreement—and Adriana slapped one of them and walked off. Leo Giovannucci saw the whole thing and he threw the first punch. After that, it turned real bad." He leaned toward me. "Listen, they're all bad news. But be especially careful around that *vagaboom*, Leo Giovannucci. He's no good."

"Oh, yeah," a voice said behind us. "You think so, old man?"

Primo sighed and, without turning, said, "Hello, Leo."

I swiveled around.

Leo Giovannucci, a heavy-set guy with tattoo-riddled biceps, looked like a human battering ram. His bald head was sleek and blunt, and it had enough bruises and scars to suggest he mostly used it to knock doors down.

Except battering rams didn't sway as if they were at sea.

"You," he said, jabbing a stout finger at me as he rocked

to the left and then leaned to the right. "My sister warned me about you. Stay away from her. Stay away from me. And —" He stepped so close to me I could smell his reek of cheap cologne and booze. "—stay away from Adriana."

His eyes, as bloodshot as they were, showed the same flinty grayness as Linda's. In the photo I'd found online, Adriana had brown eyes. Another way she stood apart from her siblings.

I put my hands up. "I don't want any trouble. I just want to make sure Adriana's all right and—"

"Stay. Away."

He jabbed at my chest, but the effort was too much. Apparently his liquid dinner hadn't done much for his balance, because he teetered to the side, throwing a hand out to grasp a barstool. He steadied himself. Then hauled himself over the stool and grabbed hold of the bar.

"Bourbon," he demanded.

Jerry gave him a long look, one eyebrow raised.

"Bourbon," Leo barked. "Now."

Jerry shrugged, turned and grabbed a bottle of Maker's Mark, then filled a shot glass. He pushed it across to Leo, who grabbed it and threw back his head, swallowing the drink in one gulp.

He set down the empty shot glass with a thunk.

"Another," he said.

Jerry filled the glass.

A person with a healthy appreciation of their own unbroken nose would've backed off, but I was determined to find Adriana. So I said, "Leo, you really don't have any idea where Adriana is?"

"No," he muttered.

"She apparently got a ride from the Romano home."

"Yeah," he said. Something about the tone was strange,

though. Not combative. He seemed to realize it himself and corrected it: "Yeah, so what if she did? She, uh, probably took a taxi."

"No," Primo said. "She didn't take a taxi."

"Maybe she didn't like your taxi," Leo said, peering over at Primo. "Maybe she took a better taxi."

"Maybe. But this is my town. Trust me. If another taxi drives around Carmine, I find out."

"Whatever," Leo mumbled and stared down at his shot of bourbon.

I considered that "yeah" he'd uttered earlier. It had almost sounded like a confirmation. Linda had also acted strangely when I mentioned Adriana getting picked up.

A hunch inspired me to tell a little lie.

"Leo, there's no point lying. Someone saw you driving from Cedar Hill that day, and there was a woman in the passenger seat."

Leo's shoulders tensed. He said, "That ain't true."

Primo and I exchanged glances, and he gave me a barely perceptible nod. Then said, "You know, Leo...I was the one that saw you. You were driving away from Cedar Hill, heading out of Carmine toward I-80."

Leo turned and faced us with a triumphant smile. "See, that's where you're wrong. I was driving the other way. How could I be going on I-80 when I was heading down Old Quarry Road? I stopped close to the Old Quarry Trail, doubled back, and then drove past the Old Mill on my way home. So how could anyone see me anywhere near I-80, huh? Tell me that."

He stared at us for another 5 seconds with that triumphant smile before it dawned on him what he'd said. He let out a low groan and turned back to his bourbon.

"You don't know nothing," he muttered. He downed the

shot. Then fumbled his wallet out of his pocket and dug out a crumpled $20 bill. Jerry gave him his change and Leo swept it up, not even leaving a buck. He staggered toward the exit.

"I hope he's not driving," I said.

Primo sighed. "Good thing I like my job."

He slid off his stool and followed Leo outside. It wouldn't be the first time Primo had taken a drunk's keys from him and given him a ride home, free of charge.

I turned to Jerry.

"Tomorrow, I'd better go check out the Old Quarry Trail," I said. "What do you think, Jerry?"

Jerry's beard parted in a smile. He gave me a thumbs up.

10

"I thought the Old Quarry Trail was closed," I said.

Nat nodded. "It was. Part of it collapsed, and it was considered unsafe. Most of it's either gone or overgrown. But you can still find parts of it..."

Nat stepped past a tree and the sapling branch he'd held back whipped me in the face.

"Hey," I complained.

"Sorry."

I pushed forward, rubbing a hand where my cheek burned. This morning, the hike had felt like an off-trail survival course. It didn't bother Nat. Cheerfully, he sent us through a city block's distance of thorny brambles that tore relentlessly at my jeans. We had to tightrope walk over a fallen log to avoid marshy ground. Then he had us clambering over slippery stepping stones to cross a creek. He managed it with the grace of a ballet dancer. I slid and sunk my sneaker into ice-cold water. Twice.

"See? Told you I'd find it."

Nat grinned as he pointed at the ground ahead of us.

The trail, if you could call it that, might once have been

wide enough to accommodate two people. But nature had reclaimed most of it, turning it into a narrow, weedy line that meandered through the undergrowth.

Shaking water from my shoe and flexing my cold foot, I said, "If Leo dropped Adriana off near here, she must know the woods well. I wouldn't have found this trail, even if I'd spent hours out here."

"Either she knows the woods well," Nat said. "Or someone else does."

I glanced at him, pushing my shoe back on and retying my laces. "You think she came to meet someone?"

He shrugged. "Why else would she come to the woods? Linda's suggestion that she went to the airport makes a lot more sense. Unless she came to meet someone."

I agreed. But who would Adriana run to? If she'd gone to stay with Linda or Leo, her brother wouldn't have dropped her off in the woods. Linda claimed Adriana didn't have a lot of friends. Could it be a lover? Was that why she left Mikey?

Nat pushed branches aside as he moved down the path. I followed him, racking my brains for ideas about who Adriana might have contacted.

Suddenly, Nat stopped.

"What's—?"

"Shh..." he hushed me.

Up ahead, the trees thinned as the terrain rose toward a ridge. In the distance, a man in camouflage gear flitted in and out of view.

Nat turned to look at me, his eyebrows raised in a silent question.

I nodded. "Let's see where he goes," I whispered. "But we have to keep our distance..."

We crept forward, trying to be as quiet as possible.

Which wasn't easy, since old sticks and pine cones littered the ground, crunching and cracking underfoot.

The man in camouflage climbed the ridge and vanished over the top. Nat sped up, and I did, too. We left the Old Quarry Trail, jogging over the leaf-strewn terrain as we tried to catch up with the stranger.

At the top of the ridge, I stopped behind a tree, trying to catch my breath. Nat stood behind another tree nearby.

I peeked around mine.

The man stood halfway down the other side of the ridge, below us. Baseball cap low on his head. Sunglasses. Beard. Backpack over his shoulders, its camouflage print blending with the rest of his outfit.

He was studying a map. From where I stood, I couldn't see the details on the map, only that it was one of those topographical maps that show you the elevation in irregular circles and kidney shapes. Too fancy for me. Unless it's a tourist map with little cartoon renditions of sights, I get lost.

The guy used a pen to circle an area on the map and cross it out. Then he pocketed the pen, folded up the map, and continued to trek down the ridge and into the gully below.

"Nat," I hissed, and he turned to look at me. "Isn't this where we—?"

He nodded. "Close. Half a mile from here was where we found the hunter."

"Come on," I said. "Let's see where this guy goes."

We set off down the ridge and into the gully. I tried to keep from running down the incline, but my legs desperately wanted to break into a run. Instead, I disturbed rocks and pine cones and leaves. It sounded like an elephant stampeding.

Somehow, Nat reached the bottom as quietly as if he'd floated down.

He gave me a wry look.

"What?" I said, frowning, knowing full well why he was giving me that look. "I wasn't raised by foxes and elves in the woods, or whatever made you this quiet."

He chuckled. "I wish."

We followed the gully until it opened to an expanse of woods with less dense tree growth. In the distance, a deer stood frozen, staring toward us. Then it moved away.

"Where did he go?" I whispered.

"Don't know."

Nat moved forward, heading out of the gully, and turning this way and then that, looking for sign of the stranger. I followed him, doing the same.

But the woods were empty and quiet.

Still, something made me feel like we weren't alone. Like someone was watching us. The little hairs on the back of my neck tickled, and I turned and looked upward, just in time to see the man in camouflage back up on the ridge.

He was looking down at us.

"Nat," I mumbled. I grabbed his arm and tugged at it.

But before Nat had turned around, the stranger ducked behind a tree. I expected him to appear on the other side, moving away from us. But he didn't. It was as if the tree swallowed him up.

"He was there," I said, pointing. "Now he's gone."

"Who was it?"

"You didn't recognize him?"

Nat shook his head. Nat knew almost everyone in Carmine. If he didn't recognize the guy, he must be an outsider.

"Whoever he is," I said, "I bet he's got something to do

with Adriana. And I don't like it. I've got a bad feeling about this."

The bad feeling might have something to do with being near the place we found the dead hunter. Or it might have something to do with Adriana Romano walking into the Carmine Woods near the Old Quarry and vanishing. Gone. Ten whole days ago.

11

I called Chief Tedesco and left a voice message on her phone, asking her to meet me at Moroni's for a coffee. We needed to talk. The guy in the woods had rattled me. Why was he hiking through the woods and marking off a map? And why so secretive?

It all made me imagine the worst: What if Adriana's disappearance was more serious than people thought?

After Nat dropped me off, so he could get back to work, I stepped into the bakery and saw that Chief Tedesco hadn't arrived yet. But a cluster of customers stood waiting by the counter.

"Bernie!" Angelica called out as she handed a customer a box. "How's the investigating?"

Before I could tell her, I stopped myself.

"What's this?" I asked.

The glass counter had been rearranged. The rainbow cookies weren't next to the pizzelle, which weren't next to the pignoli anymore. Everything had been moved to the side, and arranged in smaller mounds, to accommodate an entire shelf of glass containers with something layered and creamy covered in chocolate powder.

"Tiramisu cups," Angelica said. "Lily's idea."

Lily emerged from the back carrying a tray of more cups. But since the glass case was full, she arranged them on top of the counter.

"Uh, Lily," I said. "I don't think that's a great idea. They should be refrigerated…"

Lily beamed at me. "Not at the rate they're going."

Angelica grabbed four tiramisu cups and placed them in a cookie box, which she sealed and tied a ribbon around. Then she handed it to the customer, who smiled.

"Angelica," the customer said. "You've outdone yourself again."

"Oh, it's Lily who's outdone herself," Angelica said and put an arm around Lily, giving her a squeeze.

Something squeezed my heart, too. But it wasn't a good feeling.

Wait a sec. Was that jealousy?

Come on, Bernie. You can do better than that.

I joined the line and waited my turn. This was the right thing to do. I forced myself to smile and say, "Lily, I'd love to try your tiramisu. I bet it goes well with coffee."

"It absolutely does," Lily said, and turned to the espresso machine. "Caffè lungo, right?"

"Right."

She knew my favorite coffee. Like I was a regular. Not part of the team anymore. It felt like a little stab to my heart.

I found a seat near the back, and a few moments later, Lily brought me my coffee and my tiramisu cup. Meanwhile, more and more customers were joining the line. Lily hurried back to serve them.

From behind the counter, Angelica laughed. "Lily, I

guess everyone in Carmine's talking about your tiramisu cups. I swear they're selling better than my cannolis."

I winced, and then reminded myself that I should be happy for Lily. I wanted her to thrive.

Just not in my job...

But it wasn't my job anymore.

I stuck a spoon into the cup and dug out a bite of tiramisu. The sponge cake and mascarpone covered in powdered chocolate filled my mouth. Any secret hope I'd had that it would taste bad fled my mind. I closed my eyes as sugary pleasure filled my entire body.

"*Mamma mia*," I muttered.

It was heavenly. And incredibly rich. But Lily was smart: she'd made the cups small, so you could indulge in this sinful dessert as a treat alongside your coffee without then guilting yourself into some silly diet.

I sipped my coffee, the bitter flavor mixing perfectly with the sweetness of the tiramisu.

I glanced over at Lily and Angelica, working side by side in a professional harmony I could never offer. I sighed. Lily was thriving. I was happy for her.

Really, I was. If I had to commit to one true calling—tiramisu or detective work—the choice was clear. And Lily's vocation was obvious, too.

But her success only underscored how important this assistant investigator job had become—if I failed, I didn't see how I could return to Moroni's. That door was closed.

12

"Have you tried these new tiramisu cups?" Chief Tedesco asked when she sat down. "They're delicious."

"They're amazing," I admitted. "But can we talk about Adriana Romano?"

Chief Tedesco smiled. "We can talk about anything. I managed to leave the OPS agent behind. I said I had personal business to attend to—lady's health stuff—and that I'd be taking an early lunch break. The guy's been stuck to me like glue, but he didn't dare to question that."

She let out a sigh.

"He's giving me an ulcer. He's demanding to know every little detail, and not just about the dead hunter in the woods, but every single ongoing case. Questioning how I'm running my investigations, demanding I call in the state cops to trawl the woods for clues to the hunter's death. Honestly, he's overstepping, and that's an understatement. But I'm worried that if I complain, he'll make my life a living hell. I've got another week of this audit. I just have to suck it up and endure..."

She ran a hand through her hair. Her bowl cut had more streaks of gray than I remembered.

"Anyway," she said, turning her attention fully to me, "what's new on the Adriana case?"

I told her about my encounter with Mrs. Romano, Linda and Leo Giovannucci, and the man in the woods.

She nodded as I summarized the events of the past couple of days. Then said, "I'd worry more about the Romanos and Giovannuccis than some hunter wandering the woods with a map." She clicked her tongue and shook her head. "You've walked right into a hornet's nest, Bernie. The Romanos and Giovannuccis spent years fighting each other."

"But Adriana Giovannucci married Mikey Romano."

"Yeah, and it wasn't a popular choice. But by then Joseph Romano—that's Senior, not Junior—and Don Giovannucci were both dead. And since they started the war, maybe Mrs. Romano, the only surviving parent, thought it was worth allowing the marriage. After all, it sort of served as a peace treaty."

I opened my notepad and jotted down this new information.

"Why were they fighting in the first place?" I asked.

"Long story short? Joe and Don were business partners. They owned G&E's Auto Sales, Carmine's number one car dealership. Joe and Don were best friends and the two families were like one. The kids grew up together."

"Sounds wonderful."

"I guess it was—until Joe caught Don doing some creative accounting. Skimming the books. So Joe tossed him out. And by the time the lawyers sent everyone their invoices, Joe got the whole kit and caboodle and Don and his family had to start over."

"Yikes."

"Yeah, yikes. But, of course, there are two sides to every story, and Don insisted Joe set him up. That it was a plot to steal the business from him. Either way, it split the families, transforming them from best of friends into worst enemies."

"But then Adriana and Mikey fell in love?"

"Yup, just like Romeo and Juliet. Although that's the first and last time anyone's going to compare Mikey to Romeo. Anyway, it makes sense. Adriana and Mikey grew up together. Both of them are quiet, introverted types, who didn't have a lot of other friends in school. So they stuck together, even after their families split."

I nodded. That did make sense. Just because the parents hated each other didn't mean the kids—who'd grown up together—would feel the same way.

"What about the other kids? How do they feel about each other?"

Chief Tedesco grimaced. "Not good. Joe and Enzo, I believe, follow the family line more closely than Mikey did. And Linda and Leo blame the Romanos for all their bad luck."

"And what about—" I flipped through my notepad to find the name of the other Giovannucci. "—Bud? What's his story?"

"Bud Giovannucci served in the military. Some kind of special ops, I believe. But he was discharged, and then vanished. He went off-grid."

"Linda seemed to think Adriana had stayed in touch with him."

Chief Tedesco shrugged. "Maybe. But I've never heard anyone mention where the guy lives, and I get the sense that he's distanced himself from the family."

"Linda suggested Adriana might've gone to stay with Bud."

"That would make sense. Mikey Romano told me he got a call from Adriana a few hours after she left, and she said she was staying with family."

"He what?" I stared at Chief Tedesco. "I can't believe Mrs. Romano didn't tell me that."

"She might not know. Mikey seemed pretty cagey about it. Like he didn't want to share the information with me, either. But then Mikey's always been a little awkward."

I cocked my head, studying her. "It's been 10 days since Adriana left her home, and there's been no word from her. But you don't seem worried."

"Bernie, look at it this way: Mrs. Romano has those boys of hers locked up in that big house on Cedar Hill. If you were married to Mikey and had to live with Mama Romano, how long would you last?"

"About a minute."

"Right," she said. "So, I'm counting on her turning up, probably halfway across the country. Maybe she's with her brother Bud. Or someone else. There's an ex-boyfriend from college that, according to Mikey, was obsessed with her. He called him a "nutcase." But that doesn't mean Adriana wouldn't turn to him in a marital crisis. Who knows, maybe they're back together again." She shook her head. "I don't have time for soap operas. I've got my hands full with this dead hunter and—"

The bell above the door jingled and Chief Tedesco glanced toward the entrance. She stiffened. Then muttered an Italian curse.

"Agent Mabley," she said. "How nice to see you."

The OPS agent towered over us. He frowned.

"I knew it," he said. "I knew you were sharing details of the investigation with a civilian."

"I'm having a cup of coffee with my friend," Chief Tedesco said. "And some tiramisu. You should try some. It's delicious."

Agent Mabley's frown only deepened. He hugged his clipboard to his chest. "No, thank you."

He checked his wristwatch. "Do you always take such long lunch breaks, Chief Tedesco?"

"Well, I—" she said.

He tsk-tsked, shaking his head. Then flipped a page on his clipboard and made a note. He said, "I'm beginning to see a pattern emerge for the Carmine PD. A pretty sloppy pattern."

I glanced at Chief Tedesco. Her hands, one grasping her spoon and the other clutching her tiramisu cup, clenched with white-knuckled anger. But her crooked frown suggested a different emotion: genuine worry.

13

The next day, Nat and I hiked out to the Old Quarry Trail again. I didn't share Chief Tedesco's confidence that Adriana would just turn up. And I worried that the man in camouflage we'd seen had something to do with her disappearance.

I was sharing my worries with Nat.

"And I've been thinking, what if the dead hunter is connected to Adriana's disappearance?" I said. "What if Adriana witnessed the hunter getting shot, and she's off hiding somewhere, afraid for her life?"

"I've been thinking, too," Nat said as we moved down into the gully where we'd seen the stranger before. "The guy we saw yesterday had a map. He was marking it off. Why? He must've been looking for something."

"Yeah—" I struggled over a rock, slippery with moss, "but what?"

"I don't know. Maybe he lost something and he's not sure where he dropped it. So he's going back over the path he took, methodically searching for it."

That didn't seem implausible. And my mind raced over

what he might be looking for: his favorite thermos...or maybe the weapon he used to kill the other hunter. But speculating didn't get us closer to solving the mystery of who he was.

For a while, we moved through the woods in silence. A series of stepping stones took us over a marshy area. Then the terrain hardened and rose again.

I was rounding a giant oak when I saw him.

I froze.

For a second, I heard Nat's steps behind me. Then he stopped, too, and I knew he saw what I saw.

Straight ahead. About 300 yards away. The man was wearing the same camouflage outfit he'd worn yesterday, and he was walking away from us. Every now and then, he stopped and looked left and right, like he was surveying the area, and then he'd bring out his map and make a note with a pen before continuing his trek.

"Come on," I whispered, and gestured for Nat to follow.

I set down my feet as carefully as I could, stepping on rocks as much as possible, avoiding the leaves and twigs that would rustle and snap.

Then the guy didn't just turn right and left, but swiveled around, and Nat and I ducked behind a tree.

My heart thumped in my chest.

"Did he see us?" I whispered.

Nat peeked around the tree. "I don't think so. He's marking his map again. Wait a sec. He's done. Now he's walking on."

I let out a breath, relieved. If we could follow him without being spotted, he might lead us to his car, and with a license plate number, we'd have a clue to his identity.

We followed the man for what felt like an eternity. A full hour. And miraculously, he didn't see us. But then his attention was always on the terrain ahead of him and what lay immediately to his left and right. And his map, of course.

After a long time, he stopped, and Nat and I hid behind a tree again. He dug out a phone—it must've vibrated silently in his pocket—and spoke for a while. He was too far away for us to hear. After he put away his phone, he opened his map again and marked it. Then he strode off to the right, moving with a swiftness that suggested he had a new purpose.

"That phone call..." I whispered to Nat. "He's had a change of plans."

Nat nodded. "Let's see where he goes."

To keep up with the stranger, we sped up, and it meant being a little less careful about where we stepped. I mostly kept to the rocks, but occasionally, I danced across a mess of sticks and leaf litter, wincing each time my footfall set off an explosion of crunches and snaps.

Annoyingly, Nat moved as quietly as a ninja.

Another half hour passed in this way, and then the stranger vanished over a ridge. I was worried we'd lose him. So I sped up.

I'd almost broken into a jog, and I came over the ridge far too fast. I stopped. My shoes made a hard crunch in the leaf litter.

Crap.

I jumped to the side, taking cover behind a tree.

My heart hammered in my chest.

Nat, more careful, crept up the ridge and made sure to hide his approach behind the tree.

"Did he see you?" he whispered.

I shook my head. "Don't think so. But there's a cabin down there."

"A cabin? This far out in the woods? You're allowed to build homes out here—I mean, it's all protected."

He peeked around the tree. "But yeah, that sure is a cabin. One of those hunting shelters, I think. And the guy's standing outside. Oh, hold on. He's got a visitor. Someone's walking up a path toward the cabin."

Nat drew in a sharp breath.

"Bernie," he said. "You'd better take a look. You're not going to believe who's here..."

Nat stepped back, giving me space to look. I peered around the tree.

Down below us, among the trees, lay the log cabin. The man in camouflage stood outside the door to the cabin, arms crossed. This close to him, I could see him better. But that didn't give me much of an idea of his appearance. His big, bushy beard and sunglasses dominated his face.

But who was the visitor? How bizarre. It was a person in a blue postal service uniform, walking up the path toward the cabin. What was a USPS delivery driver doing in the middle of the woods?

Then my heart leaped into my throat. I knew that gait. I knew her. It was my point of contact in the witness protection program.

U.S. Marshall Roberta LaRosa.

14

"Holy cannoli," Nat said. "Roberta, your WITSEC contact, is down there?" He let out a low whistle. "Why do I feel like this investigation just got a lot more complicated?"

"Because it did."

If Roberta was back in Carmine, it could only mean trouble. But did that trouble have something to do with Adriana's disappearance? More likely, it had something to do with the dead hunter. Down below, she'd disappeared into the cabin, with the man in camouflage following close behind.

"You think Mr. Camouflage down there is in witness protection?" Nat asked.

"Could be," I said. "That would explain why Roberta's here." I peered around the tree again. "I wish we could be a fly on the wall and hear what they're talking about."

"Well, come on then," Nat said with a grin. "Let's be flies."

This was one of the many things I loved about Nat. I never had to convince him to do a little sneaking around. It must've been the bad influence of too many Nancy Drew mysteries during childhood—not to mention binge-watching *Silver & Gold* hundreds of times.

We crept closer to the cabin. Luckily, the one window on our side was shuttered, so no one would see our approach. I only hoped there was another window that was open, or else we wouldn't see or hear anything.

The ground sloped down to the cabin, where it leveled off, before the ground continued to fall at a less steep incline in the direction Roberta had come from.

Nat and I jogged to the cabin, hunched low, the way Eve Silver and Adam Gold always did in the TV show when we were approaching the bad guy's hideout. Except in the show, we had guns and that special invincibility to enemy fire that all mainstream TV detectives seem to enjoy: all the heroes needed was "one clean shot," but a dozen machine guns couldn't hit them. No one ever accused *Silver & Gold* of being too realistic.

With my back to the cabin, I moved around the corner. But the window on the other side was also closed, its shutters fastened.

"What do we do?" I whispered.

Nat, who'd stuck close to me, shrugged. "I don't know."

Just then, I heard a snap and a snick, and then the shutters flew open. I jumped back, pressing myself flat against the cabin wall.

"There," a voice said from within. "Let's get some fresh air in here."

I knew that voice. It was Roberta.

When I was sure that she—or Mr. Camouflage—wasn't going to look out of the window, I crept closer.

"What a mess," Roberta said within. "Did they take anything?"

"I can't be sure," a man's voice said. "But I don't think so. I think they came for this." Something rustled, like he was pulling a piece of paper out of his pocket. "But I keep it with me at all times."

"Smart thinking," Roberta said. "What's this by the door?"

"Oh, that? I'll show you. A tripwire I set up. It's what alerted me on my phone that someone broke in."

Now, the door was on the other side of the cabin. If they were looking at something over there, maybe I could risk peeking through the window.

I straightened up. Then crept closer to the window, careful not to knock the shutters. And careful not to step on a twig.

I raised my head to the open window and looked in.

And suppressed a gasp.

Inside, the cabin was in complete disarray. Papers strewn across the floor. The pillows on a couch tossed aside. Pens from a cup spilling off a desk. Piles of stuff—books, magazines, a desk lamp—thrown on the floor.

Mr. Camouflage was crouching down, picking up items. A wireless keyboard for a computer, a microphone—one of those I'd often seen vloggers use online—and a blanket that he tossed back onto the couch. Roberta was helping him tidy, picking up the books and putting them back onto a book shelf near the door.

To the right was a wooden counter with a metal sink. But no faucet, just the sink. A little camping stove stood next to that, flanked by a few canned goods. Plus, a couple of tin cups and a thermos, too.

"What in the world is this?" Roberta said, holding up what looked like a vinyl record made of gold.

Mr. Camouflage shrugged. "Golden Record."

Next to me, Nat made a sound. I glanced over at him. He was grinning and made a thumbs up. I shook my head, resisting the urge to sigh audibly. This wasn't the time to geek out about his history trivia.

Roberta picked up another object, this time from the bookshelf. It looked a lot like a toy flying saucer.

"At least the burglar didn't crush your models."

"Amazingly, no," Mr. Camouflage said. "In fact—" He turned to the desk and picked up a model of a rocket ship. "—they've managed to tear up everything else, but my models have survived. That's at least something to be grateful for."

Roberta nodded. "Another thing we can be grateful for is that they showed their hand. This suggests the person is desperate."

Mr. Camouflage scratched his beard. "And is that reassuring? Desperate means dangerous."

"Fox, we don't know what happened yet. But we'll find out."

The man—apparently named "Fox"—nodded, and then turned around. I ducked. My stomach tightened into a knot. He'd looked straight at me. Or at least he'd faced me. With those sunglasses of his, I couldn't tell where he was looking.

"I'd better get going," Roberta said.

I gestured at Nat. It was time for us to leave, too.

15

The encounter in the woods had been a breakthrough. But to what? We knew the man in camouflage was named Fox. And we knew Roberta La Rosa was involved.

I also knew that I had to respect Roberta's need to remain incognito. Her postal worker uniform—and the USPS truck she often drove—provided her with an important cover for the witness protection work she did.

I couldn't risk exposing her.

So, as I spent the rest of that day asking around Carmine about a man named "Fox," I avoided mentioning the cabin or Roberta. I made up a story about finding a cap he'd dropped in the woods, with his name written inside the lining.

I asked Father Bruno at St. Joseph's, the folks at Martinelli's Market, Rusty at Rusty's Auto Repair, Joanna at Parisi & Parisi, Dan Russo at Russo's Realty, even Nat's boss, Mrs. Viola.

But no one had heard of a man named Fox in the Carmine area.

That evening, Nat and I met for drinks at the Old Mill. As we settled onto stools at the bar, Jerry pulled the taps to fill a couple of pints of India Pale Ale for us.

I shook my head. "It's hopeless," I said. "No one knows who this Fox guy is."

"I know. I checked our records at the historical society, and there was a guy named Wolf who lived by Lake Carmine for years, but no Fox. And that cabin? It's not supposed to be inhabited. I checked. It is a hunter's shelter. You can store supplies for the day or spend a night, but the guy had a desk and computer and all kinds of gear."

"Do those shelters even have running water and electricity?"

"Nope. But this Fox guy seems to have turned it into a home. Complete with flying saucer models."

"Weird," I said.

"Not weird," Jerry said, placing the beers in front us. "Not if it's Fox Roswell."

For a moment, Nat and I were stunned into silence. It wasn't every day that Jerry actually spoke. He preferred gestures, grunts, or simply blinking to communicate. But besides that, he'd actually identified Fox.

"Fox Roswell?" I said. "Who's that?"

Jerry waggled his fingers at me. "Phone, please."

I handed him my smartphone, and he opened a browser, tapped something, and then handed the phone back to me. The top search result had brought up "Fox Roswell's You Know UFO." I clicked on the link. It was a channel with hundreds and hundreds of videos, each one obviously dealing with UFOs, extraterrestrials, and conspiracy theories about government cover-ups of "alien contact." In the description, it described Fox Roswell as "a nomad investigator of extraterrestrial phenomena, roaming North America in search of the truth."

"He's a UFO kook," I said.

Jerry shrugged. "Or expert," he said.

I clicked on one of the videos, and turned the phone so the three of us could watch.

In the video, Fox's face, with that unruly beard, filled most of the screen. He wore his sunglasses, even though the video must've been recorded at night. Behind him, one of the windows to the cabin stood open, and the dark trees outside were barely visible.

It was a recorded livestream from a week ago, in which he talked about alien abductions in Brazil and similarities to cases recorded in Romania, Mongolia, and Liberia.

After watching a couple of minutes of it—the talk went into excruciating, almost scientific detail—I swiped out of the video and chose another, much older livestream. Fox looked the same, but the background was different. A nondescript motel room, with a TV on the wall and a bed behind him with an ugly yellow-and-brown bedspread. He talked about a theory that the U.S. military had sent genetically modified humans on a Voyager vessel into deep space. No tongue in cheek.

I picked another video. A recent one.

Again, he was in the cabin the Carmine Woods. This one was about government coverups in the United Kingdom, and a supposedly secret council established by the European Union to keep "first contact" under wraps.

Nat said, "He clearly knows a lot about UFOs and E.T.s."

I detected a note of respect in his voice and gave him a skeptical look.

"What? Even if I don't believe everything he says, I can

still admire his attention to detail. Oh, whoa! Bernie, stop the video."

I'd been looking at Nat and missed whatever he saw.

"Go back a few seconds," he said.

I moved the video back a few seconds and hit play again. Fox was talking, his big microphone visible in the foreground, his sunglasses bobbing up and down as he droned on and on about EU law related to engaging with aliens.

Then, in a flash, someone passed behind him. A person crossing from one side of the cabin to the other.

I stopped the video again. And moved it back a few seconds again. I changed the playback setting to slow it down. And then replayed it.

Fox's voice, slowed down to a crawl, sounded like some bizarre animal muppet. His mouth moved with camel-like exaggeration. But my attention was on the background. All three of us—Jerry, Nat, and I—leaned closer to my phone's screen.

Then it happened. The person moved into view, her progress slowed down enough for us to recognize her, despite the way she ducked her head as she hurried past Fox.

Goosebumps broke out on my arms.

"That's her," I said. "That's Adriana Romano."

16

The next morning at dawn, Nat and I lay on the ridge overlooking Fox's cabin. This time, we'd brought binoculars. And snacks. A bag of dried mango. Because potato chips or pretzels were impractical on a stakeout—you didn't want anything making too much noise.

"This mango..." Nat said, chewing, "...is silent but deadly. Keeps sticking in my teeth. Next time, we bring donuts. They're silent but easier to chew."

"Shh..." I said. "Here he comes."

Down below us, Fox had stepped out of the cabin. He closed the door behind him. Then checked his map before turning toward us.

"Crap," I said, and Nat and I scurried down the ridge.

We found a big tree that had fallen and we crept under the trunk. I tried to still my breath. But between that and my heart thumping in my ears, I felt like I was advertising my presence for miles.

Fox would find us.

I dug my fingers into my thighs, gritting my teeth.

Please...please...

I wasn't sure who I was begging.

But it worked. Fox strode right past us, heading toward the area we'd spotted him in yesterday.

"Early bird," Nat whispered after he'd passed us. "I wonder what worm he's trying to catch."

"Adriana?" I suggested.

"Judging by the video, he already did."

Last night, we'd watched dozens of Fox's videos, hoping to catch sight of Adriana again. But there was only that one from nine days ago. Two days after Adriana had left home.

I'd slept poorly during the night. I kept thinking about calling Chief Tedesco. Wanting to. Then not wanting to. I could trust Tedesco with anything, but with Agent Mabley looking over her shoulder, I worried that it might compromise whatever Roberta was working on. So around 3 a.m., I came to the conclusion that Nat and I should follow Fox to learn as much as we could about him.

Now we slid out from under the tree trunk and we crept after Fox. Before we got to the area where we'd seen him last time, he veered off to the north, heading for higher ground. The land rose steeply, and rocky bluffs shot up from the leaf-strewn ground.

After trudging across unmarked terrain for half an hour, Fox found a well-worn trail and began to follow it.

"Where are we?" I asked Nat, my sense of direction completely thrown off by following Fox.

"We're near the Balcony, I think."

"The Balcony?"

"It's a cliff with a beautiful view. Sort of like the Overlook. And it used to be where people would meet for romantic trysts."

"Trysts? What, did this happen two hundred years ago?"

"Ha ha," Nat said. "Very funny. You know what I mean."

"Hooking up?"

"Yeah, hooking up. And you know, two hundred years ago, couples probably hooked up there, too."

"They trysted," I said and winked.

Nat slapped my arm. "You've made your point."

I grabbed Nat's sleeve, tugging at him to stop. Up ahead, Fox stood still. He was studying his map again.

Nat said, "See those two cliffs opposite each other? The tall one on the left is the Balcony. There's a kind of gorge that runs between them. Looks like Fox is heading in."

Ahead of us, Fox disappeared into the gorge. Nat and I talked over what to do next. If we followed him into the narrow space, and Fox turned around, we risked being seen by him. Nat described it as a long, tunnel-like space. So we decided to head upward instead. From the Balcony itself, we might be able to keep an eye on Fox down below.

Nat knew how to get there, and he led the way. We hiked up a narrow, winding path that was part dirt, part boulders. I wondered if the steepness and roughness had once deterred an older generation from investigating the Balcony, making it an ideal place for young lovers to meet.

At the top, I could see why it had been nicknamed the Balcony. Cliff walls on either side opened up to a wide ledge. Countless couples had carved their names into the rock. It was hard work, carving into stone, and most names were initials scratched into the surface. However, a few, more dedicated people had chiseled their entire names: *Eric + Maria, Joey + Gina 4ever*, and...

"Look," I said. "*Nat + Emma*."

Nat sighed. "Emma Francis. I can't believe she carved our names into the rock here."

"Good thing she came to terms with you two not being a thing."

"Yeah, it's no fun to have someone obsess over you."

I stepped forward, getting closer to the edge. Across from the Balcony, the other cliff rose up. Although it wasn't flat, it also looked like you could climb it.

Down below, the gorge was a rugged mess of tumble-down boulders, gnarly trees, and deep shadows.

"You see him?" Nat whispered.

It took me a while to spot him, because Fox wore his camouflage clothes, and the vegetation and rocks in the gorge were dense. And also because Fox was standing stock still.

His hands hung loose by his sides, the map still clutched in one hand. He was staring at a space between a cluster of boulders.

Something was lying between the rocks.

The realization struck me like a sharp pain to the chest. All air left my lungs. No breath left. I reached out and grabbed Nat's arm, suddenly feeling vertigo.

"Oh God..."

It wasn't something caught in the boulders below. It was someone. A body, twisted among the rocks, her long hair splayed across the stone.

And an arrow jutting out of her chest.

17

"**M**y God," I said. "It's Adriana."

My voice echoed across the gorge. Fox's head jerked up. He stared straight at us. Then turned and jumped onto a big boulder, as agile as a cat, and in a flash, he melted into the vegetation.

I expected to see him emerge from a bush and run. But he didn't. The gorge was silent. Nothing moved.

"Where did he go?" I asked.

Nat stared at the spot where Fox had stood. He shook his head. "No idea."

I dug out my phone from my pocket, no 3 a.m. doubts stopping me this time. When my call went to voicemail— "*This is Carmine PD Chief of Police Diana Tedesco...*"—I hung up and dialed again, and kept dialing until she picked up.

"*What's going on, Bernie? I'm in the middle of—*"

"Adriana Romano," I said. "We found her."

"*Oh? Where?*"

"In the woods. In the gorge below the Balcony."

"*Below—?*" She seemed to catch on, understanding the

implications, and she cursed. Then added, "*I'll be right there.*"

"Wait," I said. "There's more…"

Quickly, I told her about Fox, how Adriana had appeared in one of his videos, and how we'd caught him standing over the body before he'd vanished. But I left out Roberta.

"Nat and I will go to the cabin."

"*Bad idea,*" Chief Tedesco said. "*He may be dangerous. Stay right where you are. I'm dispatching Officers Ferrante and Fontana right away.*"

I shushed into the phone, making as much noise as I could. "Uh, sorry…shh…I can't hear you…shh…bad connection…shh…think I'm losing you…shh…"

"*Bernie, I'm not falling for that old trick. I'm—*"

I hung up.

"Let's move," I said.

"To the cabin?" Nat asked.

I nodded. "Fox must be headed there. And if he isn't, we might find evidence of Adriana's stay."

Nat and I hurried down the narrow path from the Balcony. Part of me felt a responsibility to poor Adriana—to waiting by her body. Another part of me was relieved not to take a closer look.

After a slow descent—we were careful not to go tumbling down the cliff—Nat and I sped up. We'd spent so much time creeping after Fox, it felt like such freedom to break into a run.

The first stretch, along the trail to the Balcony, passed in no time, but once the path turned and we kept going straight through the woods toward the cabin, the going got tougher. It slowed us. We'd come a long way this morning, following Fox for an hour and a half. How much of an advantage did his head start give him?

Finally, with my legs on fire and my lungs ablaze, I stopped by the fallen oak tree, resting a hand against it as I tried to catch my breath.

"Come on," Nat said, only lightly winded.

I could see that years of hiking made a difference. During my Eve Silver era, I had a personal trainer. Nowadays, it was a major victory if I restricted my cannoli intake to one ricotta-filled shell a day. Maybe giving up my bicycle in favor of a car wasn't such a good idea, after all.

We crested the ridge and, for a moment, stood looking down at the cabin. The shutters were closed. The door, too. I started to walk toward it and Nat joined me.

Halfway down the ridge, I heard a vehicle. A four-wheel-drive police cruiser came bumping up the path—which wasn't wide enough for the car—its lights flashing. It was only then I realized that a pair of tire tracks already made lines on the ground.

Someone had driven up to the cabin before.

"Oh, no," I said.

"Yup," Nat said, "here comes Chief Tedesco. And I bet that Agent Mabley is with her."

"It's not that..."

I broke into a run, flying over downed branches and rocks, until I reached the cabin door. I yanked it open.

Just then, the cruiser slid to a stop a few feet away. Chief Tedesco jumped out on the driver's side. And I barely had a chance to feel the disappointment at seeing Agent Mabley exit on the passenger's side, because I was staring into the cabin and seeing—

"Nothing," Agent Mabley said, his voice dripping with disgust. "There's nothing here."

"The place was full of his things," I said, staring into the bare cabin. In the time it took Nat and me to get here, someone had cleaned it out.

"So you say," Agent Mabley said, making another note on his clipboard. It was like oil on fire, making my anger flare up. I clenched my fists.

If he makes another note on that clipboard, I swear I'll...

Chief Tedesco must've noticed my anger. She put a hand on my shoulder.

She said, "I believe you, Bernie."

Her radio crackled to life. She tapped it, and Officer Anthony Ferrante's voice sounded: "*We found her, chief. Just like Nat and Bernie said.*"

Agent Mabley frowned. "Found who?"

I sighed. I let go of my anger. Below it hid a deep sadness. In all the excitement of the chase, I'd pushed away how I felt about finding the body. Now it came rushing over me.

My voice shook a little as I gazed down at my trembling, open hands and said, "Adriana Romano. She's dead. Shot with an arrow."

Thud!

Startled, I looked up.

Agent Mabley stared at me, eyes wide with shock. His beloved clipboard at his feet.

Then, his own voice shaking, he pointed a finger at me.

"You—you killed her..."

18

I was sitting by Officer Fontana's desk at the Carmine police department. As usual, he was listening to the radio and typing a report. Nat sat next to me.

"I wouldn't worry, Bernie," Fontana said. "That OPS guy's just like all the other pencil pushers—as soon as they see a dead body, they freak out and start calling everyone a killer."

"He thinks because we happened to find two bodies with arrows in them, we're prime suspects," Nat said.

Fontana shrugged. "The two cases do seem connected."

From one of the interrogation rooms, we could hear raised voices. Loud enough to carry through the supposed sound isolation. A few choice words from Chief Tedesco made it through: "absurd" and "unfounded" and "out of bounds." But Agent Mabley wasn't cowed. He added his own volley of words: "unprofessional" and "manipulative" and "murder-loving actress."

Nat nudged me and said, "I'm gonna go out on a limb and say he's talking about you."

"You think?"

The door to the interrogation room flew open and Chief Tedesco stormed out. She looked like an angry Greek goddess. Like she'd throw lightning bolts at you. Agent Mabley came striding out behind her, apparently unfazed.

He locked eyes with me, glaring. Then looked beyond me at someone. Something shifted in his gaze.

He checked his clipboard and announced to Chief Tedesco, "After this, I'm going to make a few phone calls within the Office of Professional Standards, and then we'll see how much longer you run this investigation."

"Go ahead and try," Chief Tedesco muttered through clenched teeth. Then looked up. Her gaze softened. "Mikey..."

Officer Anthony Ferrante was escorting Mikey Romano through the police department. Apparently having just identified the body.

Mikey's eyes were red-rimmed, his face deathly pale. Anthony offered him a seat by his desk. Mikey collapsed onto the chair and buried his head in his hands.

"Oh, Adriana," he said, and his shoulders shook.

Chief Tedesco sat on the edge of Ferrante's desk.

"Mikey," she said. "This is a hard time. I know. But we're going to have to ask you questions. We need your help to find whoever did this."

"But—" His voice caught in his throat, choking on a sob. "But I don't know."

"Let's start at the beginning. Why did Adriana leave?"

"There was a—" He paused. He dug out a handkerchief from his pocket. This guy was old school. Not a lot of guys his age used handkerchiefs. He blew his nose. Then said, "There was a fight. At the Old Mill."

I remembered Primo mentioning it.

Chief Tedesco apparently knew all about it already. "Yes,

you and your brothers were having drinks, and then got into a fight with Leo Giovannucci."

Mikey nodded. "But actually, it started without Leo. It started with Enzo." He drew in a ragged breath and let out a long sigh. "We were having drinks. Joe got a call and stepped outside. And I went to the men's room. And while we were gone, Enzo..."

He looked at us, twisting the handkerchief in his hands, suddenly embarrassed. Then he said, "Enzo made a pass at Adriana."

"I see," Chief Tedesco said.

This was big. I glanced around. Officer Fontana was frowning, looking offended. Anthony avoided looking at me, forever feeling sheepish about how he'd treated me when we dated. But Agent Mabley was the most interesting: He was gripping his clipboard tightly and staring intently at Mikey, like someone watching the cliffhanger in the season finale of their favorite show.

"Was this the first time he'd done it?" Agent Mabley asked.

Chief Tedesco shot him an angry look. A warning.

Mikey looked up. "Who are you?"

"From the state police's Office of Professional Standards," Agent Mabley said. "Just answer the question. Had Enzo done it before?"

Mikey, obviously not knowing about the Office of Professional Standards, and what Agent Mabley's jurisdiction covered, shook his head. He said, "Enzo had come on to Adriana a bunch of times. She was always complaining that he was taking photos of her. She said it was creepy."

"And what was your response?" Chief Tedesco asked, taking the reins again.

"I tried talking to Enzo, and he said she was exaggerating. It got bad for a while. Joe stepped in. He told Enzo to back off. And he told Adriana to stop encouraging Enzo. Like, you know, stop dressing provocatively and stuff."

"And how did you feel about that?"

Mikey shrugged. "I mean, Adriana did sometimes wear stuff that Momma didn't think was OK."

"I see. And what about Enzo's behavior?"

"Oh, it got much better after Joe stepped in." Mikey frowned. "Until that night at the Old Mill. And then after the fight, Adriana just left. Just took off."

"Just like that?" Chief Tedesco said. "She packed her bags and left that evening?"

Mikey nodded, but he looked down at his handkerchief, twisting it around and around, strangling it. I thought about him telling Chief Tedesco about Adriana's phone call, a fact he'd kept from his mother. What else was he hiding?

Agent Mabley stepped forward. "You're lying."

"Agent Mabley," Chief Tedesco snapped. "Please."

But Mabley didn't listen. "There's something you're not telling. Just like you initially didn't want to tell anyone that —" He paused for a beat. "—that your wife called you after she left. Well, what is it? What is it you're hiding?"

Mikey looked up, wide-eyed, like a terrified animal, cornered by a predator. His lower lip trembled.

"She left me—" he blubbered. His shoulders shook, as did his voice. "We were going to—going to leave together—but she left me."

"You were going to leave?" Chief Tedesco said. "Where were you going?"

"To the city. Away from the car dealership. Away from my brothers. Away from Momma." Mikey's knuckles turned white as he throttled his handkerchief. "It was our plan. Together. But then she left me..."

He threw his handkerchief down on the floor, his face suddenly twisting with anger.

"Why couldn't she wait? She didn't—"

The angry mask cracked. His face crumpled. He buried it in his hands again and sobbed.

Next to me, Agent Mabley said, "He did it. He murdered his own wife..."

Oh, come on, I wanted to say.

I glanced over at Fontana, remembering what he'd said about OPS guys freaking out and calling everyone a killer. But Fontana was busy looking at Mikey, frowning deeply.

Chief Tedesco was watching Mikey, too. Suspicion etched on her face.

19

The Romanos' mansion on Cedar Hill contrasted with the neighboring Victorian houses. It was built in an imposing neoclassical style, maybe even inspired by the White House, with a portico of imposing columns. Behind that rose a giant dome. All in gray stone.

The garden was mostly a lawn, so wide and free of trees that you could land a helicopter on it. If that was your kind of thing.

I rang the doorbell. A chime sounded deep inside the vault of the Romano home. My heart, which had been beating faster and faster with every step toward the door, now galloped.

An hour after I'd left the Carmine PD, Mrs. Romano had called with a simple message: "Come to my home on Cedar Hill. Now." Then she'd hung up, leaving me no opportunity to speak.

The door opened. I expected a butler or maid, but it was Mrs. Romano herself who stood there.

"Follow me," she grumbled. She turned and walked

toward a massive staircase, her low heels clip-clopping on the marble floor. "And close the door behind you."

I closed the front door and hurried after her.

The staircase rose to a landing and then curved around, rising to the floor above. We passed an alcove with a giant oil painting of a man in a suit: the patriarch, Joseph Sr., tall and lean and dark. Then we passed another alcove, but a pair of drapes shut off whatever was inside.

I followed her to the floor above. She led me down a hallway. The doors on either side had brass nameplates, like the ones I'd seen at the car dealership: Joseph Jr., Enzo, Michael.

The faint drone of music came through Mikey's door.

Guess the grieving husband is home.

I was reminded of teens listening to moody music. I'd expect Mikey's choice of music to be extremely moody at this point. Poor guy.

"So," I said, "where did Adriana and Mikey live?"

Mrs. Romano glanced over her shoulder, giving me a disapproving glare. "You can read can't you?"

So Adriana lived in Mikey's old bedroom?

It was hard enough to imagine what it would be like to marry a guy and move into his childhood home. But to then occupy his old bedroom right next to his brothers...

"This is my suite," Mrs. Romano said, and gestured for me to follow her into the room at the end of the hallway.

Holy moly.

So Mama Romano slept just down the hallway from Adriana and Mikey. No wonder she wanted to get out of here.

We entered an office with a giant hardwood desk and built-in bookshelves all around. A door stood open to a master bedroom beyond. Apparently, Mrs. Romano liked to keep her study close to her bedroom.

Apparently, she likes to keep everything—and everyone—close.

"Sit."

Mrs. Romano indicated a chair facing the desk.

She sank onto a giant office chair, placed her elbows on the armrests, and steepled her hands as she glared at me.

"I'm sorry for your loss," I said.

"My loss—" she said. "—will be if my son Mikey is accused of murder."

I tried not to show my shock. Her daughter-in-law—a young woman who'd lived down the corridor—had been found murdered, and her only concern was for her son?

She said, "The fact that Chief Tedesco is even considering Mikey as a suspect reflects poorly on your performance."

"I'm sorry," I said, confused. "I don't understand. I don't control Chief Tedesco's investigation. And since many spouses or partners are often behind murders, it makes sense to—"

"I read the news, Miss Smyth. I know the statistics. But I didn't hire you to tell me about national murder statistics. I hired you to find my daughter-in-law."

I nodded. "And I did, unfortunately, find her."

"But I also told you not to bother my son." She shook her head. "I ought to fire you on the spot. It's like I've taught my sons: If you want something done well, you've got to do it yourself."

Something heavy dropped into the pit of my stomach. Mrs. Romano reached for a phone that sat on the desk and rested her hand on it as she stared at me.

"However," she said slowly, "I don't have time to run

around playing detective. So I will give you a chance to prove your worth."

"Thank you," I muttered, feeling a child-like shame. Like being chastised by my kindergarten teacher. Or that time my parents made me apologize to our kid-hating neighbor, Mr. Boogman, for smashing the glass in his greenhouse with my ball.

Mrs. Romano said, "I want you to find the person who killed Adriana and ensure that my son is kept out of this mess."

"I can try to find Adriana's killer," I said. "But as a detective, I can't promise to clear your son's name."

Mrs. Romano picked up the phone. "Then let me call Cosimo right away."

She started to dial a number. With one call, she could end my opportunity to get started. I knew her type. She wouldn't listen to reason, and why should Cosimo trust my word over hers?

Besides, I'd met Mikey. He was a wet rag. Hardly the kind of guy who solved his marital problems with violence. The statistics might suggest that he should be a prime suspect, but if I had to make a bet...

And you do have to. Make a bet.

"Wait," I said. "No need to call Cosimo. I'll do what you want me to. I'll find Adriana's killer..."

"And make sure Chief Tedesco stays off Mikey's back? You'll protect my son?"

I bit my lip. A jittery energy ran through my limbs, a desire to jump up and stride out of Mrs. Romano's study. But like that time with Mr. Boogman, I pushed my emotions down and looked Mrs. Romano in the eye.

"I'll do it," I said. "I'll protect Mikey."

20

The next morning, I returned to the Happy Hunter. Since I'd ruled out Mikey Romano as the killer— or rather, my client had—my best bet was to take another look at the Giovannuccis. Starting with Linda.

I'd tried calling Roberta La Rosa, hoping she could shed some light on the elusive Fox Roswell. But she didn't answer.

So, I wandered down the aisles of hunting nets, tents, and decoys, wondering how I could approach my conversation with Linda. I'd better start by showing my sympathy. And insisting my sole motivation was to find Adriana's killer. How would she react to that? She might see me as an ally. Or, if she had anything to do with the crime, an enemy.

Or she could see you as Mrs. Romano's puppet...which wouldn't be so far off the mark.

I winced at the words in my head. I hated it when my inner critic was right.

But I had work to do. I silenced the voice and looked around.

No one at the counter at the back. So I drifted past racks

of hunting clothes—vests, camouflage cargo pants, hats—
and over to a massive display of bows.

I'd never seen so many different bows and crossbows.
Some of the crossbows looked like modern versions of the
medieval weapon. But others took their inspiration from
guns instead, resembling assault rifles. Some of the
composite bows looked like alien technology, with weird
handles and pulleys, while the ones labeled "recurve"
reminded me more of something Robin Hood might use.

"Can I help you?" a sales guy said, approaching me. He
wore a Happy Hunter polo shirt and a name tag that said,
"Alex." He must be in his mid-twenties. Crew cut. Acne
scars.

"Actually, I was looking for Linda..." I said.

Alex smiled. "Don't blame you. Bows and crossbows
aren't my specialty. Linda's the expert."

I hesitated for a second. Then realized this was my
opportunity.

"Yeah, I heard she knows her stuff. I'm new to hunting
with a bow and arrow, and a friend recommended I talk to
her. Is she around?"

"Not today. She called in sick." Alex made his version of
a sympathetic face, his mouth turning down in an exagger-
ated frown. "Family tragedy."

"Oh, I'm sorry to hear that."

Of course she wouldn't come to work the day after her
sister was found murdered. She must be in shock. Unless, of
course, she knew Adriana was already dead...

Alex, apparently not only to linger on sad news, bright-
ened. "But I can help you. I mean, I'm not a former state
champion archer, but I'm sure I can help you with the
basics."

Did I hear that right—state champion archer?

As I pretended to look at the display of weapons, I said, "I heard Linda was an expert archer, but I didn't realize she competed."

"Sure. She used to be the best archer in New Jersey. One of the best in the country. No bullseye was safe when she was around." He chuckled at his own joke. Then followed my eyes. "That crossbow is a good place to start. It doesn't require a lot of strength." He glanced at me. Color spotted his cheeks. "Uh, I mean, not that you're not strong."

I laughed. "I'm strong in many ways. Just not with a bow and arrow. Do you need a lot of strength to pull the bow?"

"Depends on the bow. But yeah, if you're working a traditional bow, it's going to take some practice. Depends what you're hunting, too. And how close you need to get."

I thought of the Balcony. My guess was that Adriana had been standing on the Balcony when she was shot. Then she'd fallen down into the gorge. Or the killer had pushed her over the edge to hide the body. Which meant the killer could've been standing on the cliff across from the Balcony —under 50 yards away.

I said, "What if I was, say, 50 yards from my target."

"How big a target?"

"Uh—" I could hardly say "human size." So I settled for, "—a deer."

"That would be pretty far for a bow and arrow. You also have to think about making sure you don't just maim the animal. You want a clean, responsible kill."

I shuddered, thinking of how someone had treated Adriana like a "kill."

Alex added, "A crossbow is a better option if you want to hit something 50 yards away."

I'd overheard Officer Fontana say that Adriana had been

killed with a standard arrow for a bow. I wondered if that ruled out a crossbow.

"Could I use standard arrows for a crossbow?"

"No," Alex said. "And why would you want to do that? It wouldn't be safe. Plus, it would make it harder for you."

"All right. I think I'm more interested in a bow. If I learned to handle the bow and arrow as well as Linda, could I hit a target 50 yards away?"

Alex laughed. "Good luck with that. She started when she was a little kid. But yes, if you practiced like crazy and achieved Linda's level of mastery, you could definitely take down a deer 50 yards away."

I could hear Mrs. Romano's voice in my mind: *See, I told you so. The Giovannuccis are behind all this.*

What if she was right? What if Linda Giovannucci—former New Jersey state champion in archery—killed her own sister?

21

Nat switched off the engine, turning the key in the ignition, and his ancient Honda Accord settled down with a sigh. The tie-dye dice hanging from the rearview mirror swung back and forth. On the stereo, one of his many cassette tapes of Grateful Dead concerts was playing. But now he turned the dial, switching it off.

"And if Linda isn't here?" he asked.

I shrugged. "Then we figure out what plan B is."

"I thought this was plan B."

I'd recruited Nat to check out Linda's home. But her house looked empty, abandoned, and when I rang the bell and knocked, no one came to the door. Now we'd parked down the street from Leo's place, hoping we'd find his sister there.

We walked down the cracked, potholed street. The edges of the blacktop crumbled into the dirt.

Whereas Linda's home had been a modest ranch-style home with aluminum siding in a good working class neighborhood, Leo's home lay in a woodsy area where the closest neighbor was a junkyard. He lived in a trailer on blocks, with a filthy, partly ripped awning, and several flower boxes that contained stubbed-out cigarettes but no flowers.

Two cars stood parked outside Leo's home. One was a decades-old Honda, like Nat's, but so beat-up that it looked like it belonged in the junkyard next door. The other was a new Prius.

I said, "Let's get off the street before someone sees us."

"There's a path over there, going into the woods," Nat said, pointing.

We followed the path into the trees, keeping Leo's home far enough away to our left that we wouldn't be spotted. In the distance, we could now see the back of his home. A wooden deck jutted out over a small, weed-choked back-yard. A woman sat in a deck chair. A man stood by the steps to the deck, smoking a cigarette.

"That's Linda and Leo," Nat whispered.

"Let's get closer," I suggested.

Nat nodded and put a finger to his lips.

He was right. We had to be quiet. And careful not to be seen. Leo's backyard merged with the woods, and there weren't other backyards nearby, which meant that any movements among the trees might raise suspicion.

After this case, I'm going to enroll in a forest survival and stealth course. I need it.

Nat and I moved from tree to tree, keeping low and hiding behind the trunks. As we drew closer and closer to the backyard, the voices grew clearer.

Leo said, "...you think they care? They think I'm a loser. They're gonna pin this on me. You see."

"Oh, grow up," Linda snapped. "This isn't about you."

"Right," Leo said. "Because it's actually about you."

"No, you idiot. It's about friggin' Adriana being—"

She stopped. She put a hand to her mouth and turned away from Leo.

Leo stared at her. Apparently at a loss as to what to say. Not a man comfortable with emotions. He tossed his cigarette aside. He turned and shoved his hands in his pockets.

"Bastards," he exclaimed and kicked an empty beer can, sending it tumbling across the yard.

Linda turned back toward him. "Who?"

"All of them."

He stomped up the steps to the deck, yanked open the screen door, and vanished into the trailer. The door slapped shut. A moment later, he emerged again, carrying something in his hands.

My breath caught in my throat.

He was carrying a recurve bow. In his fist, he clutched several arrows.

Linda said, "Leo, where did you get that?"

"It's my old bow. I pawned pretty much everything else, but I couldn't say goodbye to this."

He held it up to the sky, admiring it.

"It's a beauty, isn't it?"

Then he stepped down onto the grass again and strung an arrow. He aimed. And fired.

The arrow whizzed through the air and thunked into a tree.

Nat whispered, "He's not bad."

Not bad? He hit a tree about 40 yards from the trailer.

Leo smiled, clearly pleased with himself. "I still got it."

"Put that toy away," Linda said.

"You're just jealous."

"Maybe I am. And maybe I'm not such a *stuppiau* that I

think it's a good idea to be doing target practice with a bow when some bastard shot my sister with an arrow."

Leo glanced back at her. Then shook his head. "Call me all the names you want. It doesn't matter. The cops will come for me anyway, so who cares?"

Linda shot to her feet. She strode down the steps, grabbed the bow, and for a moment, they struggled over it. Then Linda yanked it out of Leo's grip.

"Hey!" he exclaimed,

"Ah," she groaned, and doubled over, clutching her right arm.

The bow lay on the ground.

Leo took a step toward her, a hand reaching out, as if he wanted to touch her, comfort her, but didn't quite dare. So he hovered over her, awkwardly.

"You all right?" he asked. "Is it the arm?"

"What do you think?" she snapped.

"It's worse?"

"It's always worse."

"Jeez. You oughta get a doctor to look at it."

Still bent over, clutching her arm, she glared up at him. "So they can operate again? And only make the pain worse?"

"But maybe this time they can—"

"Anyway," Linda said, straightening up with a grimace, still clutching her right arm, "my lousy health insurance won't cover it, so who's gonna pay for another operation? You?"

Leo rubbed the back of his neck and looked down at his feet.

Linda said, "Yeah, I didn't think so."

She turned away, walked back to the deck, and snatched up her purse with her left hand. She kept her right hand tucked against her chest. Without saying a word of goodbye, she strode around the trailer, disappearing from sight. A moment later, a car door slammed. Another moment passed and then a car drove away.

Leo picked up the bow. He nocked another arrow, aimed at the same tree, and let it go. But the arrow went wide, vanishing into the woods.

He cursed and threw the bow aside. Then stomped inside the trailer and slammed the screen door.

That afternoon, I settled into Angelica's little office in the back of Moroni's. A cup of coffee and a plate with pignoli cookies sat in front of me. And my notepad, too.

The cafe itself was so packed—Lily's tiramisu cups had gone viral on social media—that I couldn't find a seat. Anyway, I needed some peace and quiet to think.

After spying on Linda and Leo, Nat and I had grabbed mortadella sandwiches at Martini's Italian Market and eaten them on a bench in Puccini Park, discussing what we'd seen.

Now I needed to gather my thoughts and report to Cosimo and Chief Tedesco. I jotted down a list of suspects, considering everyone possible:

Linda Giovannucci
Leo Giovannucci
Bud Giovannucci
Fox Roswell

Mikey Romano
Enzo Romano
Joe Romano Jr.
Mrs. Romano

Linda had seemed like a good suspect. An archery champion could count on killing Adriana from a distance. But Linda no longer practiced archery. Nat and I had done some online searching and found an article from a few years ago that mentioned Linda's career-ending injury. These days, she could hardly use her right arm without triggering debilitating pain.

Then there was Leo. His archery skills had surprised me. I'd assumed Linda was the only archer in the family, but why should I? Linda was the oldest Giovannucci. Younger siblings often wanted to join the sports their older siblings got involved in. Leo had a history of violence. He himself seemed to understand what a good suspect he would be. But what was his motive? Why would he want to kill his own sister?

The same applied to Bud. He'd gone off-grid. But I couldn't see what motive he'd have for hurting his sister. If anything, the fact that he and Adriana had been in touch suggested that he would be a potential support, not a threat.

And then there was Fox Roswell. The UFO nut. Adriana had stayed with him. Against her will? Or did she somehow know him? When she rushed past him during the livestream, Fox didn't flinch. Hardly the reaction of a man who was holding someone hostage. And if Roberta was somehow helping him, I had to believe she wasn't protecting a murderer.

But then witness protection was full of people who'd done bad things...

I looked at the rest of the list, and I sighed. All Romanos. I'd promised Mrs. Romano to protect Mikey. But that didn't mean I shouldn't consider the others...

I grabbed my phone and called Cosimo.

"Yeah," he said, his voice muffled by chewing. "Tell me what you got so far."

I filled him in on the Giovannuccis, Fox Roswell, and then described the unusual living arrangements at the Romano home.

"Stop right there," he said. "Who's our client?"

"Mrs. Romano, of course."

"Correct. And why did she hire us?"

"Uh, to find her daughter-in-law's killer."

"Wrong. She's got a problem. Her son is grieving the loss of his wife. He can't work. She needs him—and her other sons—to carry on the family business. Right now, this murder is an obstacle to her vision for the future. *Capisce*?"

"I guess so..."

"So she hired us to remove an obstacle. Find the right killer, and we remove the obstacle."

"That's what I'm working on."

"Good," Cosimo said. "And what's Cosimo's number one rule?"

"*It's the client's way or the highway*," I repeated dutifully.

"Very good. And is it the client's way for you to investigate her family?"

I hesitated. Of course I knew what Mrs. Romano would say.

Cosimo said, "Since you're new to this, I'll help you out. The answer is *no*. She doesn't want that. And what does that mean for your list of suspects?"

An immense weariness weighed me down. Like gravity just got stronger.

"It means that I remove the Romanos from the list," I said.

"Bravo. It's true what they say—you can teach new dogs old tricks."

He hung up. I sighed. One by one, I crossed out the Romanos.

Linda Giovannucci
Leo Giovannucci
Bud Giovannucci
Fox Roswell
~~Mikey Romano~~
~~Enzo Romano~~
~~Joe Romano Jr.~~
~~Mrs. Romano~~

Then I called Chief Tedesco.

23

Chief Tedesco suggested we meet at the Old Mill for an after-hours drink. I made another call to Roberta—and got no answer—then sat at the bar, making sure the stool next to me remained free.

But when Chief Tedesco arrived, Agent Mabley was trailing her.

"I'm going to the men's room," he announced. "Can you order me a seltzer with lime, please?"

He walked away. As soon as he was out of earshot, Chief Tedesco slid onto the barstool next to me and muttered a low curse in Italian.

I said, "Doesn't this guy ever take time off?"

"He's single and married to his job, or so his tells me," Chief Tedesco said with a grimace. "Honestly, who else would marry him?"

Ouch. Chief Tedesco usually didn't get snippy like this. But actually, I thought she was being amazingly patient. If Agent Mabley followed me around all day, criticizing my every move, I would've exploded long ago.

She ordered a glass of Pinot Grigio.

"Make that two, Jerry," I said. "And a seltzer with lime."

Jerry gave me a thumbs up and got busy preparing our drinks. Meanwhile, I quickly summarized what I'd learned so far, rushing through the details while Chief Tedesco and I had some privacy.

"You seem convinced the Giovannuccis may be involved."

"Or this Fox Roswell guy."

"But what about Mikey Romano?"

Jerry served us our drinks. I was grateful for something to fiddle with, and immediately held onto the stem of the wine glass. I said, "Well..."

"Bernie," Chief Tedesco said. "Does this have something to do with who's paying your fee?"

When I didn't answer, she added, "You aren't Cosimo. He's in it for the money. But you—"

I turned to her. "I'm a thirty-something woman without a career."

"Moroni's is a good place..."

"Look at Lily—she's got what it takes to work at Angelica's bakery. I don't. And I don't think I want to. If you ask me to pick tiramisu or murder, I know what I'll choose. Chief, I've got to pursue my passion now, or find something else. Because my next big milestone is forty. And then what's next? Perimenopause?"

Agent Mabley slipped onto the stool next to Chief Tedesco, grabbed his seltzer, and took a sip.

"So," he said, "what are we talking about?"

I leaned over the bar, so I could look across Chief Tedesco at him. I said, "Perimenopause."

He stared at me, and I expected him to be embarrassed. I'd been counting on it, hoping I could scare him off. But he didn't seem moved by what I said at all. Maybe Chief

Tedesco's attempts to shake him had made him even more stubborn.

"Change of topic," he said. "Let's hear what you've learned about the Romano murder."

I turned away from him, facing forward, and took a sip of my wine. "I don't think I need to discuss that with you."

"Miss Smyth, I'm aware of your cozy relationship with Chief Tedesco. Believe me, it will feature heavily in my report. But if I discover that you two are exchanging information about an official investigation, then I'll have no choice but to report Chief Tedesco immediately to my superiors and call in the state police to take charge of this jurisdiction."

Chief Tedesco shot me a weary look, as if to say, "Yeah, this is what I've been dealing with all day, every day." But also, "Please don't make this harder for me."

I shrugged. "Fine. What do you want to know?"

I might be willing to cooperate. But I wasn't going to serve him everything on a silver platter.

"First of all—" he began.

Then I saw someone exit the restrooms at the back and a jolt shook me. I nearly knocked over my glass of wine. I caught it right before it fell, sloshing some on the bar.

"Oops," I said. "Clumsy me."

Behind Agent Mabley, Mikey was heading for a booth, apparently returning from the restroom. He weaved right and left, bumping into the booth before managing to collapse onto the seat. And then grabbing the bottled beer on the table and guzzling it.

My mind raced. Mrs. Romano's voice echoed within: "*Make sure Chief Tedesco stays off Mikey's back. Protect my son.*" If Agent Mabley saw Mikey, Chief Tedesco would be forced to react, and somehow I knew it would get back to Mrs. Romano that I'd been with them.

"Here's what I know," I blurted out, cutting Mabley off. "Linda Giovannucci used to be state champion in archery. But she injured herself..."

I hurtled through the details about Linda's injury and Leo's proficiency with a bow and arrow.

Agent Mabley sipped his seltzer, looking unimpressed. "I don't see a compelling motive. So I'm not interested in the Giovannuccis."

Who cares who you're interested in?

I looked to Chief Tedesco, wanting her to protest. But she simply gave me a little shake of the head. I didn't like how this OPS agent used his power to control Chief Tedesco. And I didn't like how much he was meddling in the investigation—it was starting to seem like he was way out of line.

He continued: "I'm interested in Mikey Romano. As we all know, a spouse or partner is most likely to be the killer. The two families were at war, and yet Mikey lured Adriana to him. That suggests a level of manipulation that's typical of abusive partners. So, tell me, you've been close to the Romanos. What have you observed about the family?"

"Nothing."

"Nothing?" Agent Mabley sighed. "Do I need to remind you about my report?"

"Look, Mrs. Romano doesn't want me—or anyone else— meddling with her family. That's the truth. She hired me to investigate her daughter-in-law's death, because she's concerned about her son. She didn't hire me to look into her family life."

"But you must've observed something."

"They're rich," I said with a shrug, trying to feign a

casual but firm belief. "Aren't all rich people more or less alike?"

He drained his seltzer. "If you believe that, you'll never make a good detective. Come on, Chief. I've heard enough."

Chief Tedesco gave me a long-suffering look. She drained her wine. Then said, "I'm tired, Agent Mabley. I'll be heading home for an early night."

"Me, too," he said. "Early bird catches the worm."

And the two of them walked away. The door closed behind them.

No, Agent Mabley. I slipped off my stool, grabbed my wine glass, and headed toward Mikey's booth. *This time, the late bird catches the worm.*

24

"Mikey," I said, facing him across the table in the booth. "What're you doing here?"

"What does it look like?"

He tipped the beer bottle to his lips, but it was empty. Fortunately—or maybe unfortunately—he had another one ready. A cluster of empty bottles stood on the table next to two untouched ones.

"It looks like you're exercising your right to drinking your brains out. But why not do this in the privacy of your own home? I imagine you have some pretty good Scotch at that mansion of yours."

He looked down at the table. "You wouldn't understand."

I was hoping he would understand me, so he'd get out of here. Go back home. If I had to call Primo and escort Mikey home, I would do it. I wouldn't feel great about it. I was supposed to be a private investigator, not Mikey's personal assistant. But it would no doubt meet Mrs. Romano's expectations.

"Nobody understands," he muttered before taking another big swallow of beer. "Adriana and I—"

Oh, how I wanted to get up and walk away. Oh, how I wanted to ignore the invitation to ask a question. Mrs. Romano had made it clear: I shouldn't be interested in her family.

But I was. I couldn't help it.

I said, "What, Mikey? What about you and Adriana?"

He tore at the label on the beer bottle. "We were going to start over in the city. I was finally going to pursue my dream. I illustrate comics. I've even sold a few under a pen name." He shot me a frightened look. "You can't tell anyone, okay? It's a secret. Because if Momma found out..."

"I won't," I promised. "Cross my heart and hope to die."

He sighed. "Adriana believed in me. She believed we could live a different kind of life. On our own. In our very own apartment." He looked up at me, nodding at me wide-eyed, as if he wasn't fooling around—as if the idea of living in an apartment with your wife was the most radical idea ever. "She found a studio apartment in the Bronx. She even found a job as a receptionist at a design agency. She saw it as a way to get close to the work she really wanted to do. Art and design. And it would give us enough income to get started."

He took another slug of beer.

"She believed in me..." he said, and his shoulders shook as he began to sob. Tears streamed down his face. "But I didn't—I couldn't—"

"Couldn't what?" I asked, leaning forward.

"Go home," a voice said above me, and I looked up.

Enzo Romano was leaning against the side of the booth, a smirk on his face. But it was Joe who'd spoken.

"Go ahead," he said. "You can go home now, Bernie. Thank you for looking out for our brother. But we'll take it from here."

He put a hand under Mikey's arm and hauled him out of the booth. Mikey resisted a little, but not much, and by the time Enzo had his other arm, he allowed himself to be escorted away.

Enzo glanced back at me. "If you stick around, I can come back and buy you a drink."

"I'm good, thanks."

He winked at me. "Some other time, then."

Ugh. His sliminess made my skin crawl.

But as I watched the two older brothers escort Mikey out of the Old Mill, it was a different feeling that overtook me. A hard, cold thing spreading in my stomach, like an ice-cube melting.

I brought out my notepad and opened to the page with my list of suspects. If Mikey and Adriana wanted to flee home so badly, and Mrs. Romano's priority was keeping the family together, then at least one of the people on my list had a motive.

Mrs. Romano.

But she was crossed out. And I knew I couldn't even begin to consider her a suspect. Not in a million years.

25

The encounter with Mikey had exhausted me. It wasn't a physical exhaustion as much as an emotional one. Just looking at my list of suspects, with half of them crossed out because their last name was Romano, made my head ache.

Like Chief Tedesco, I needed a quiet night at home. A quick dinner, then straight to bed.

I'd taken my canary yellow bike to the Old Mill. The bike ride across town added to my exhaustion, and by the time I swerved onto Lampedusa Lane and my little ranch-style home came into view, I was considering skipping dinner and going straight to bed.

Then I hit the brakes.

My back tire skidded to the side as I came to a halt and I set down my feet.

Up ahead, a truck stood parked in my driveway. But not any kind of truck. It was a USPS truck. And I knew for a fact that the postal service didn't deliver at this time. They didn't park in driveways at night, either. Which could only mean one thing—or rather, one person.

I opened the front door and called out.

"Roberta?"

I headed down the hallway to the kitchen. The kitchen table came into view, and I froze.

A man was sitting at the table, a bottle of root beer in front of him.

Not just any man.

"Fox Roswell," I said.

He gave me a nod. He wore his sunglasses and a baseball cap. Between those two accessories and his massive, unruly beard, his face was mostly hidden, as were any facial expressions.

At least his hands were on the table, one holding the bottle, the other resting. Could he be hiding a crossbow under the table? If he had a gun, how quickly could I turn and run out of the house?

Then I heard a toilet flush, the door to my bathroom opened, and Roberta came striding out.

"Bernie," she said, as if we were in the middle of a conversation, and it hadn't been ages since we'd seen each other, "sit down and let's talk through this case."

She wore a baseball cap, too, and a pair of sunglasses. But maybe in a gesture of how much we'd been through together, she took her glasses off and met my gaze.

"You've got questions," she said. She opened the fridge and held up a bottle. "Root beer?"

"Uh, sure."

Roberta sat down at the table, next to Fox. She indicated the chairs across from them and pushed a bottle of root beer across to where she expected me to sit.

"Please, we've got a lot to cover."

"Did you get my calls?" I asked, as I eased myself onto a

chair. I grabbed the root beer, grateful for the cold drink after my bike ride.

Roberta nodded. "Of course. But I already knew you'd contact me before you called."

Fox said, "I saw you and your friend creeping around the woods, and I called Roberta. She insisted that you weren't a danger."

"Me?" I said. "A danger? You're the one that—"

"I'm the one that was looking for Adriana," he said testily. "Which would've been a heck of a lot easier if I didn't have to sneak around, worrying about intruders like you."

Intruders? Where did he get off calling me an intruder? He was the one creeping around the forest like Big Foot.

"Oh, yeah? Well, how about you tell me why you were stalking Adriana?"

"She was staying with me. She went out one night and never came back."

"Staying with you?" I said, and snorted to show how little I believe him.

I was bone-weary. Tired of playing games. And maybe I was taking it out on Fox. Or maybe he deserved it.

"And how willing a guest was she, really? Did you give her one phone call, like she was in custody, and then—"

"Whoa there, Bernie." Roberta held up a hand. "Let's back up."

"Yes, let's." I crossed my arms. "First off, who are you, Fox, and why was Adriana staying at your cabin?"

Fox drew in a deep breath and then let out a long sigh. He peeled off his cap. Then his sunglasses. And he stared at me with a pair of gray eyes.

I dropped my arms and leaned forward, staring at him. I knew those gray eyes.

"You're a—"
"Giovannucci," he said, nodding. "I'm Bud Giovannucci."

26

"Bud Giovannucci and Fox Roswell..." I said. "Of course. The brother that went off-grid. But that Adriana was still in touch with. That's why she came to stay with you."

"She had no other place to go," Bud—aka Fox—said. "In fact, when she learned that I'd set up shop in the Carmine Woods, she begged to visit me. But I told her it was too risky, in case *they* were watching."

I glanced at Roberta, and she gave me a barely perceptible shake of the head. Basically, *don't ask*.

Bud said, "But when she walked out on the Romanos, I couldn't turn her down. She called me and I told her she could stay with me." He scratched his beard. "Maybe if I'd still been in Nebraska or Arizona, she wouldn't have gone. Maybe then—"

He looked down at his hands. Tears gathered in his eyes. He swiped a hand at them, wiping them away.

"I'm so sorry," I said softly, my heart aching for him. Linda and Leo's reactions hadn't been so straightforward, but as I watched Bud try to catch his breath and keep the tears at bay, I understood: He'd loved his little sister.

He said, "She said she'd move on within a few days. She said she had a place to stay and a new job, both in the city. And that Mikey was going to join her. If she could only convince him. When she left that night, I thought she was going to meet him. Then, when she didn't come back, I worried they got her."

"Who?"

"The Men in Black. Covert government groups that want to suppress knowledge about alien contact," Roberta said, speaking quickly, and casting me another quick, warning glance. Turning to Bud, she said, "Anyway, tell Bernie about this."

She placed a sheet of paper on the table. It was a copy of a photograph. I recognized the place—the cliff rising like a tower from the forest floor.

"The Balcony," I said. "What is this?"

"A photograph," Bud said. "It came with a letter. This is a copy of both."

Roberta said, "I delivered the original anonymously to the Carmine PD earlier today. We think the killer may have sent this letter, inviting Adriana to the Balcony. Then, after her death, he returned to the cabin to get this back."

"He?" I said.

Bud nodded. "It's pretty incriminating."

I looked at the sheet of paper. Next to the photograph of the Balcony was the copy of a brief letter. It was printed or typed. It spoke of a "desperate need" to see Adriana, suggesting they meet at "the special place."

I know you don't love me. I know you

think my behavior is "inappropriate." But I
want to be a friend to you. That's all I'm
asking. I want to help you however I can.

The letter was signed "E."

I looked up. First at Roberta, then at Bud.

"Who's 'E'?"

Then something clicked in my head. A photograph. What had Adriana said? That he was always taking photos of her, and it was kinda creepy?

"I see it now," I said. "'E' is for Enzo."

27

The U.S. and Italian flags fluttered in the morning breeze as I crossed the Romano Auto Sales lot, heading toward the front door. Rows of cars lined the side of the building, and as I passed them, I spotted Enzo talking to a woman.

Before arriving, I'd hoped he would be busy with a customer, so I could take a look around his office. It looked like this was my lucky break. He had his back to me, and he was deeply engrossed in his conversation with the woman.

"I don't know what I did," she was saying as I casually strolled behind them, hoping Enzo wouldn't notice me. "And I've tried everything to get the trunk open."

"Not a crowbar, I hope," Enzo said with a smile.

He was leaning on the car. Leaning toward her in a flirtatious way.

"No, silly," she said, and swatted his arm, apparently enjoying his attention. "But I really do need to get my stuff out of the trunk, so I can get to work."

Enzo winked. "I'll have this open in no time. See, there's

a trick to opening trunks without a key. A secret only the Romano boys know."

She laughed a don't-be-silly laugh that had a hint of oh-keep-going in it. He turned away from her, and my heart jumped, expecting him to see me. But he immediately bent down to examine the trunk.

I sped up, reached the front door, and slipped inside.

Jenna was watering plants by a cluster of sofas. Another lucky break. She had her back to me, and I didn't hesitate.

Walk quickly...and with confidence. No one will see me.

I strode across the carpeted reception and, as Jenna shifted to another plant, watering that, too, I continued to head straight past the desk...

Please, please, Jenna, don't look up.

...and down the corridor to the offices, out of her sight.

Another lucky break: Joe's door was closed. I stepped into Enzo's office and turned the handle gently, closing it with only the softest of clicks.

My heart hammered in my chest. Although the walk to Enzo's office hadn't been strenuous, I felt winded.

No one had seen me. I couldn't believe my luck.

Sometimes you make your own luck.

Maybe that could be Cosimo's Number Two Rule.

After my meeting with Roberta and Bud last night, I'd been restless. Restless to take a closer look at Enzo. I couldn't keep crossing out the Romanos when the clues pointed so clearly toward the middle brother.

Yes, it might cost me my gig as private investigator. But I wasn't going to help Mrs. Romano cover up a murder.

Now was my chance to find something—anything—that tied Enzo to Adriana's death.

I looked around.

Enzo's office was tidy. A long, low bookshelf ran along

the left-hand wall, and apart from a few trade magazines about cars, a Hot Wheels toy car on a tiny pedestal, and a few framed photographs, it was noticeably bare.

Actually, photography seemed to be a recurring theme. Giant framed prints hung on the walls, featuring nature scenes and iconic sights, like the Verrazano Bridge and the Statue of Liberty. But none of them looked like the run-of-the-mill posters you could buy for $10. They looked like originals.

I moved around his desk. Apart from the computer screen, keyboard, and mouse—and a vintage call bell placed near the edge as a decoration—the surface was clean.

I opened the top drawer. Inside was a book: *The Ultimate Professional Photographer's Guide.*

I opened another drawer. It contained stacks of photographs held together with rubber bands. The top one showed a woman staring off into the distance, rays of sun filtering through her hair.

I picked up the stack of photos, undid the rubber band, and flipped to the next one.

Another woman. This time at a supermarket. She was reaching for a box of cereal on a top shelf, stretching, and her shirt was lifting a little, exposing her midriff.

The next photo had caught a jogger—also a woman—who'd stopped to tie her laces, the sweat on her shoulders glistening in the sun.

The photos were good. Professional. Even artistic. But above all, they were singularly focused on one thing: women. It was like a catalogue of the male gaze, each shot an intrusion on a private moment. Enzo definitely hadn't asked for permission to take these photos. It was part of the appeal, the thrill, the—

When I saw the woman in the next photo, my stomach twisted.

Adriana was bent over the desk in the reception, one hand hooked into a strand of hair, the other curled protectively around a glossy magazine. I couldn't see the contents of the magazine. The focus of the photo was on the nape of her neck, and a chill ran down my spine as I thought of Enzo standing behind Adriana, watching her through the viewfinder of the camera.

I had to get this photograph to Chief Tedesco. I had to—

The door clicked opened. I shoved the photos back into a stack and forced the rubber band back into place—pulling it too hard. It snapped. The photos slipped from the pile in a neat cascade, like I was performing a card trick.

Enzo filled the doorway.

He froze. But only for a moment. Then he slipped inside and pushed the door closed behind him, setting his back against it. Trapping me.

"Well, well, well," he said. "And here I thought we hired you to dig up dirt on the Giovannuccis, not rummage through our stuff."

"I was just…"

I bent and grabbed the photos, bunching them together. My heart too small for my chest. I didn't have a good cover story. I didn't have any story at all. And Enzo knew it.

I straightened up, holding the photos in my hands.

"You were just looking at my personal stuff," he said.

No purpose in lying. If defense was pointless, then offense might be better.

"You took photos of Adriana without her permission. You basically stalked her."

He smiled. "So I flirted with Mikey's wife and took a few

snapshots. Big deal. She was too good-looking for him, anyway. It was only a matter of time before she left him."

"And she was going to leave him for you?"

Enzo snorted. "I was having some fun, that was all."

"Was meeting her in the woods fun?"

His smile vanished. He frowned. "What're you driving at?" He took a step toward me. "Now, listen here. If you think you're gonna pin this murder on me, you're wrong. I've got nothing to do with Adriana. Nothing."

"You came on to her at the Old Mill. It was what made her move out."

"So?"

Enzo continued toward me. I instinctively backed up, my legs hitting his desk chair. I glanced behind me. A window that didn't open. No way out.

He said, "She and Mikey were always whispering. You think I didn't realize they were talking about leaving?" He reached the desk and started to creep around it, stalking toward me like a predator cornering its prey. "So I thought maybe she needed to kiss a real man before she took off." His face split into a grin. Not a smile, but a showing of teeth. "And what about you? You ever kiss a real man?"

I clenched my fists, ready for a fight. Then caught sight of the call bell on the desk.

I drew back my fist, and Enzo flinched, pulling back and throwing up a hand to protect his precious face.

But I didn't punch him. I slammed my fist down on the call bell and it dinged loudly. He jumped back, almost as frightened by the sound as by my raised fist.

I whacked it again, and again, and it dinged and dinged.

"Stop that!" he yelled.

The door flew open.

"What's going on?" Joe said, glaring at his brother. "What did you do this time?"

28

"**B**ut Joe—"

"Out, Enzo," Joe ordered from behind his desk. "Before I lose my cool."

Enzo muttered a curse and retreated to his own office, slamming the door behind him, like a truculent kid.

Joe let out a breath as he stared at the closed door with a world-weary resignation. Then he extended a hand toward me and indicated one of the chairs in front of his desk.

"Please, Miss Smyth, sit. Coffee?"

My heart was still racing after the confrontation with Enzo, though less wildly. I automatically said yes to coffee, even though I had no idea if I really wanted it. Joe turned to an espresso machine in the corner of his office and began fixing us both Americanos.

"I apologize for my brother," he said. "This isn't the first time I've had to check his boorish behavior." He glanced back at me. "I hope you're all right."

I nodded. I was struck by the contrast to Enzo—and Mikey, for that matter. Joe came across as well-mannered and a little old-fashioned. A gentleman.

He handed me a cup of coffee with a perfect layer of crema on top. I thanked him and took a sip. Not bad.

He sat down behind his desk. Like Enzo's, it was clean and tidy, except for a single decorative element: one of those perpetual motion models with metal hoops and balls representing the solar system. Back in high school, I'd found one at the Sharper Image and got it for my boyfriend. He told me it was the best gift anyone had ever bought him for his birthday. He told me he loved me. The next week, I caught him making out with Jenny Jensen, captain of the cheerleading squad.

Unlike Enzo's office, Joe's felt like it was devoted to the business. The walls had a few posters, all showing cars. The bookshelf was crammed with car magazines as well as a few paperback books about auto repair and ownership.

Joe sipped his coffee, then put down his cup and said, "Let's cut to the chase: Enzo didn't kill Adriana. He couldn't have. At the time of her death, we were all at home—Enzo, Mikey, our mother, and me. We've gone over this with Chief Tedesco." He cocked his head, studying me. "But you must've had a good reason for taking a closer look at my brother."

I hesitated. I didn't know how much I could reveal. Of course, I would eventually report everything to Mrs. Romano...

Joe said, "I understand your hesitation. But although hiring you was my mother's idea, I'm her right hand. You can tell me."

"All right," I said, accepting that if Enzo had an alibi, then I'd need to level with Joe. Besides, I was relieved to see that he was mad at his brother, not me. But I couldn't divulge details that might compromise Chief Tedesco's work

—or Roberta's. So I said, "Adriana received a message inviting her to the Balcony, where she was killed."

Joe frowned. "A message? You mean an email?"

I shook my head. "A letter."

"I see. And this letter—it somehow implicated Enzo?"

"It contained a photograph of the Balcony and a letter signed 'E.'"

Joe nodded. "I understand why you might suspect Enzo." He took a sip of coffee. Then added, "But it's all wrong. The photograph seems like something Enzo might do. But he's not a letter writer. Enzo would call. Or simply show up. And even if he did write to Adriana, he'd simply sign his name. My brother is a lot of things, but he's not subtle."

Now that he said it, I could see his point: Except for the photos in the drawer and the way he surreptitiously took shots of women, Enzo didn't strike me as the sneaky type.

Joe's face had collapsed into a deep frown. He steepled his fingers, touching his lips as he thought.

"But I wonder about that 'E'..."

He dropped his hands and pulled open a drawer. He extracted a pile of letters and set them on the table.

"I thought these were ancient history. Irrelevant. So I didn't share them with Chief Tedesco. But I can see I might've been wrong not to do so."

"What are they?" I asked.

"Letters to Adriana from an admirer. An ex-boyfriend from college, who wouldn't take no for an answer. He was obsessed with her. He kept hounding her. After Adriana married Mikey, he seemed to back off, but then the letters started arriving at our house. Adriana got upset—and a little scared." He tapped the pile of letters with a long finger. "It's my job to protect my family. So I collected the letters before Adriana could see them and I hid them here, in my office.

As far as Adriana and Mikey knew, the guy had stopped writing."

Joe picked out a letter from the pile, unfolded it, and read a section aloud: "*I can't handle it. I need to see you. This is killing me. You're killing me.*" He raised an eyebrow at me. "It goes on and on. He's clearly crazy."

"And you think he's the 'E' who invited Adriana to the Balcony?"

Joe shrugged. "It's possible. He usually just signs his letters 'E.' But Adriana referred to him as Eric. Also, I kept some of the envelopes with the return address..."

He handed me an envelope. And there was his name along with his address. My whole body turned icy cold.

"Eric," I read, my mouth going dry. "Eric Mabley."

29

By the time Nat and I walked into the Carmine PD a couple of hours later, I was holding a manila folder with evidence. It was Nat's idea to gather details before confronting Mabley, and we'd struck gold. Before going to Chief Tedesco's office, I stopped by Officer Fontana's desk to ask him for a favor.

"With pleasure," he said. "I'll go check right away."

Then Nat and I barged into Chief Tedesco's office without knocking.

"Bernie, Nat," she said, eyebrows shooting up with surprise. "What's going on?"

Agent Mabley frowned. He'd been in the middle of a sentence.

"This is a private meeting," he said. "I'm surprised you think you have the authority to interrupt us."

I ignored him. I slapped down the folder on Chief Tedesco's desk.

"Read this," I demanded.

"What is it?" she asked.

"It's about Agent Mabley."

He reached for the folder, but Chief Tedesco got to it first. She flipped it open. And frowned.

"Rutgers Archery Club?" She looked at Agent Mabley. "You were on the varsity team? You never mentioned that."

"Hardly relevant," Agent Manley snapped. "In fact, this is highly inappropriate. This needs to end now. I won't—"

"Look at who else was on the team," Nat said, and Chief Tedesco flipped the page.

Her eyes widened. "Adriana Giovannucci."

Agent Mabley went quiet.

I said, "Adriana Giovannucci and Eric Mabley were more than just teammates. They were dating. Until Adriana ended it."

Agent Mabley's face had gone rigid. He clenched his hands into fists in his lap. But he still said nothing.

Nat said, "So, you see, Eric Mabley had a strong motive —unrequited love—and the means to kill Adriana with a bow and arrow. Plus, he was conveniently in Carmine when she left Mikey..."

"That's not true," Mabley said. "It's the other way around. I got myself assigned to Carmine when Adriana disappeared. I was worried and came to help. I—"

"You had a bow in the trunk of your car." Officer Fontana stood in the doorway. He wore latex gloves, and in his hands, he held a recurve bow. "Funny thing for an OPS agent to be carrying around."

Mabley turned in his chair, his eyes wide with horror.

"No," he said. "I didn't—that's not mine—I've never—"

Chief Tedesco got to her feet, and with a barely suppressed look of satisfaction, she said, "Eric Mabley, I'm arresting you on suspicion of murder..."

Mabley shot to his feet. "I didn't kill Adriana. I would never hurt her." He pointed at Fontana. "And someone planted that in my trunk. I haven't owned a bow since college. I gave it up after Adriana left me. My love of archery withered when—"

Snap. Chief Tedesco had hooked a handcuff on one of his wrists. Now she gently, but firmly, bent his arm around until she could fasten his other wrist.

"I'm warning you—you're making a terrible, terrible mistake," Mabley said, but his voice had lost all authority. "Please...you're making a terrible mistake."

Chief Tedesco smiled. "I don't think so. I think I'm closing this case."

30

"You came this close to being fired." Mrs. Romano held up a hand, measuring a short distance between her thumb and index finger. "After Enzo told me about how you were snooping around his office, I was about to call Cosimo. But Joe intervened. He said Enzo had misbehaved, and that you had found the real killer."

We were sitting in her study in the Romano mansion on Cedar Hill. I summarized the events leading to Eric Mabley's arrest for murder. She didn't ask any questions, and even rushed me through my report.

She said, "I'm not interested in all the details. That's for you and the police to worry about. All I need to know is that this debacle is over, and that my family can continue to focus on what's important."

Apparently, Adriana's death wasn't important. Mrs. Romano really gave mother-in-laws a bad name. But I kept my mouth shut.

"You can tell Cosimo he can send the invoice in the mail." She got to her feet. "But in the invoice, I would like all the details. Don't think you can pad it with pointless expenses." She wagged a finger at me. "I'm no fool."

She escorted me to the door and we walked down the corridor, past her sons' bedrooms. We headed down the stairs, and the giant oil painting in the alcove of Joseph Sr. came into view. A cleaner, busy vacuuming the stairs, had pulled back the drapes covering the other alcove, the one closer to us. Inside it was another large oil painting. It showed a bunch of kids playing a game of—

I stopped. "What's this?"

"What does it look like?" Mrs. Romano said. "It's a family painting."

"They're doing archery."

"Obviously."

Seven kids. One of them was firing an arrow at a target, the arrow suspended in midair, just about to hit the bullseye. Another kid stood by his side, bow held in her hands, ready to go. In fact, they all held their own bows and arrows. All seven kids. The painter had done a good job portraying them—good enough for me to recognize them.

"Those are your boys," I said. "Joe's firing the shot. And that's Enzo behind him. That's Mikey. They're with the Giovannuccis. That's Adriana next to Mikey. Linda's waiting by Joe's side. And Leo and Bud are standing together."

"So?" Mrs. Romano said. "Before the Giovannuccis tried to scam us, our families were close. The kids grew up together. In fact, they did everything together. In hindsight, it was a bad idea. It was what brought Adriana and Mikey together."

And it was what taught them all to shoot a bow and arrow. I thought of what Eric Mabley had said—that he hadn't owned a bow since college, and that he'd given up archery after Adriana broke up with him. What if he was right—what if we'd made a mistake and arrested the wrong guy?

"Well?" Mrs. Romano said. "Are you coming? I don't have all day to stand around. Least of all to look at that old painting. When you own a family business, you can't afford distractions. Time is money."

I followed her down the stairs and she led me to the front door. The door stood open. Another cleaner was working here, polishing the doorknob.

"Thank you, Mrs. Romano," I said. "This has been a great opportunity and I—"

She waved a hand and turned around. "Send the invoice."

She walked back into the mansion, vanishing down a corridor. Maybe to the kitchen or a living room. The house must have dozens and dozens of rooms. You could easily spend time in this house without knowing which family members were home. And which were out.

I hesitated.

Then said, for the benefit of the cleaner, "Oh, rats. I left my bag in Mrs. Romano's office. I'll just go grab it."

I slipped back inside. And crept back up the stairs.

31

I began with Enzo's room. What if "E" didn't stand for "Eric"? Mrs. Romano would've insisted all her boys were home the day Adriana was killed. But how could she know? And what if Joe had been protecting his brother and lied about his alibi? After all, Joe had said that it was his job to protect his family.

Unlike his tidy office, Enzo's bedroom was stuffed to the gills with gear: cameras hanging with their straps hanging on wall hooks, tripods, battery chargers, lenses. But also stacks of photography magazines and books. Printed photos lay scattered across a desk and a bed. Posters and photos—some framed, others simply tacked on—covered every inch of the walls.

I shuffled through some of the photos. More shots of women. I opened the drawers in his desk. Pens. Paper. An empty notebook. Old film rolls. More printed photos.

I checked under his bed. Nothing. No letters or other evidence anywhere connecting him to Adriana's death.

I left his bedroom and peeked down the corridor. Mrs. Romano's study door stood open. No sign of her. I could hear the vacuum going, the cleaner still working on the staircase.

I hurried into Joe's room.

Joe kept his room tidy. But unlike in his office, he didn't keep any magazines or books on cars. It occurred to me that none of the Romano boys seemed crazy about cars, despite their vocation in auto sales.

While Enzo had his photography, Joe seemed interested in science. At least he had rows and rows of books on astronomy and stars in his bookshelf. And on his desk, on top of a newspaper spread, lay a half-finished model of a rocket ship. A pair of tweezers sat next to a tube of glue and a box full of plastic pieces. It looked like it would take incredible discipline and attention to detail to finish it.

I opened a drawer. Hidden inside wasn't some shameful collection of erotica. No, just a novel by Ray Bradbury: *The Martian Chronicles*. I dug beneath the novel. A notebook filled with quotes by famous astronomers and astronauts, a postcard showing a golden record used as a bookmark. Funny how I kept encountering golden records. Otherwise, there was nothing of interest.

I looked around the room. I checked under his bed. Nothing.

Leaving Joe's room, I checked the corridor again. Still no sign of anyone. Good. I had one last Romano boy to look into.

I slipped into Mikey's room.

Unlike Enzo and Joe's rooms, which contained single beds, this one had a queen-sized bed. No doubt a concession for the married couple.

The room was a mess. Clothes strewn on the floor. A single sneaker overturned, the other member of the pair nowhere in sight. Piles of comic books tilting and toppling over: *The Walking Dead, X-Men, Batman*. Also collector issues in slipcases. One of them caught my eye: a comic called *Hawkeye*, featuring a masked superhero wielding a bow and arrow.

Then I caught sight of something on the wall, in between a poster of Superman and one of Indiana Jones: a beautifully crafted wooden bow. Next to it hung a quiver with arrows.

I approached it. I was tempted to touch it. Then held back. It might reveal important fingerprints.

"Miss Smyth."

I jumped and then spun around.

Mrs. Romano stood in the doorway, glaring at me.

"I ought to call the cops on you," she said.

But she didn't. Instead, she called Cosimo.

32

"One rule," Cosimo said, and threw up his hands. "One simple rule, and you go and break it. And you do it *after* you've solved the case."

I squirmed in my seat. This was worse than when I'd been yelled at for smashing Mr. Boogman's greenhouse. Because Cosimo was right: I'd messed up. Big time.

"And is it because you have this brilliant insight into who the real killer is? Like Columbo does in the final scene of each episode?" Cosimo paused for effect. He chewed on his cigar. Then shook his head. "Oh, no. Because the guy you insist is the killer—the victim's husband—turns out is lousy at archery. Hopeless. Everyone agrees. Mikey Romano can't hit a target if it's a mile wide."

"I didn't realize..." I muttered.

"You didn't realize." Cosimo took the cigar stub out of his mouth and leaned forward, his eyes bugging. "It's your job to realize."

He shoved the cigar back into his mouth.

"Mrs. Romano fired us. She refuses to pay the fee. She says she may choose to sue. So, you leave me with no choice..." He sighed, shaking his head. His voice dropped. He sounded almost remorseful. "I can't hold onto you, Bernie. Doesn't matter how much I owe Angelica. You're bad luck. And I've got enough of that already."

I nodded. I pushed myself out of my seat, my body feeling as heavy as lead.

"I understand," I said. "I appreciate what you did for me. The opportunity you gave me."

Cosimo shook his head and muttered something about being a sap for giving people opportunities.

I headed for the door.

My chance to prove myself as an investigator was over. Mrs. Romano had made sure of that. Actually, I myself had made sure of it. My intuition that Eric Mabley was innocent, and that the murder was somehow tied to the Romanos, had backfired. And now that the whole thing had blown up in my face, I knew deep down in my bones just how wrong I'd been.

Mikey didn't kill Adriana. Mikey was guilty of not standing up to his family and sticking by his wife. But he'd never kill his wife. He'd loved her.

I opened the door and paused, intending to offer one last apology to Cosimo for letting him down. When I turned, the weak sunlight filtering through the grimy windows flashed against an object on the wall.

A golden disc.

Just like the one I'd seen at Bud's cabin. Just like the one I'd seen on the postcard stuck inside Joe's notebook.

"Cosimo," I said.

"Now what?" he grumbled.

"What is this?"

"The Golden Record, of course. Don't they teach you anything in school these days?"

Vaguely, I recalled something Nat had said. It had been when Officer Fontana had been listening to the quiz show on the radio. Something about spacecraft carrying a record with songs, including Chuck Berry's "Johnny B. Goode," far beyond our solar system.

An image came to me: a desk ornament of a solar system made of medal, the hoops and balls swiveling endlessly.

I closed the door. "Cosimo, is the Golden Record a thing among science fiction and space enthusiasts?"

"*Mamma mia*, you've got a long way to go as an investigator. Of course, it is. It's part of a direct effort to make contact with aliens."

My heart did a little somersault. "So, someone who likes this might also be obsessed with astronomy, space travel—maybe even UFOs?"

"Sure." He narrowed his eyes and rolled the cigar from one side of his mouth to the other. "Where're are you going with this?"

I grinned, my smile so wide it hurt my cheeks. "I'm going back to Carmine. And you're coming with me."

33

"The Romanos are in a meeting," Jenna, the receptionist, informed us: Cosimo, Nat, and me. "You're welcome to wait. Would you like coffee?"

Nat smiled. "That would be great. I'll help you carry."

They moved toward a coffee machine to the far left of the reception desk. Nat immediately began talking about cars and what Jenna thought would be a good one for him to buy. Keeping her distracted.

As soon as Jenna's back was turned to us, Cosimo and I hurried down the corridor to the offices. Mrs. Romano's office door at the end was closed. No doubt where the family was having a meeting.

Joe's office stood open.

"How fast can you work?" Cosimo asked. "I don't do computers."

"You don't do computers? But these days so much of investigation involves computers."

He frowned. "Well, if you turn out to be right about this, you can take care of all my computer tasks. But let's see..."

I settled into Joe's desk chair and moved the mouse.

Luckily, he didn't password protect his computer. It sprang to life. I was also hoping he occasionally "wasted" time at the office on his secret passion.

I opened his browser and clicked on "settings." Opening the browsing history brought forth a long list of entries. I let out a breath of relief. He hadn't cleared his cache. Scrolling down the list, I could see every website he'd visited for the past 90 days.

"I don't see how any of this can be evidence of anything," Cosimo grumbled.

"Oh, it's evidence all right…"

I brought out my phone and snapped photos of the long list of sites. Many of them were related to astronomy or science fiction. Joe often visited NASA.gov. He'd spent significant amounts of time reading sci-fi stories on *Clarkesworld Magazine*'s website. He belonged to online forums where people shared their dreams about traveling beyond the stars—whether in fictional worlds or in real life.

A portrait of a frustrated man was emerging. Like his brothers, Joe had been forced to bury his passion for space in favor of the family business. Mr. and Mrs. Romano had a plan for their boys, and the widow had kept her husband's vision alive by sticking rigidly to one rule: the family business came first.

Joe, the dutiful elder son, had complied. And he'd become his mother's right hand, enforcing her rule. So when Adriana left and tried to pull Mikey with her, Joe stepped in.

"And bingo," I mumbled to myself, "here's the proof."

I clicked the link in the history, and it brought up a video. The livestream recording of Fox Roswell talking about UFOs. And Adriana rushing by in the background.

"This is it?" Cosimo asked me, looking over my shoulder. "The smoking gun?"

"This is it." I took another photo with my phone. "Ironic, isn't it? Joe probably never realized who he was watching all this time. Fox Roswell was his old family friend, Bud Giovannucci. So imagine his surprise when he saw Adriana."

The door clicked shut, and I looked up.

Joe stood by the closed door. "Put down your phone and back away from my computer, please."

I shut the browser. Then set down my phone on the desk, tapping the screen twice to activate an app.

I folded my arms across my chest. But I didn't move from the chair. "You recognized her, didn't you, Joe?"

"Yes, I did. And yes, it was a surprise. And a relief. I'd been trying to figure out where she went."

"You tried to stop her."

"Of course I did," he said. "Once I knew what Adriana and Mikey had planned—Mikey couldn't keep his mouth shut, of course—I tried to talk them out of it. He was easy. She was—" He grimaced. "—stubborn."

I said, "So, once you knew where she was, you sent her one of Eric Mabley's letters and a photo of the Balcony you stole from Enzo's room, hoping to lure Adriana out. But you were running a risk. Adriana had cut ties with Eric."

Joe shrugged. "She was desperate. She'd turn to almost anyone for help. And I found one of Eric's letters that offered to help her—as a friend. It was the best I could do."

"And it worked. You lured her to the Balcony."

Joe took a step toward us. "I'd like you to step away from my computer now. I need to erase that browser history."

Cosimo said, "And destroy the evidence? But we've basically heard you confess."

"It's your word against mine. I think you'll find our family lawyer can easily crush a sleazy, small-time private investigator and his barista assistant." He shook his head. "I told Momma not to get a detective involved, but she thought she was doing what she needed to do to protect our family. Ironically, it's had the opposite effect. Despite my efforts."

I said, "You mean your efforts to frame Eric Mabley?"

"He arrived at just the right time," Joe said, nodding. "It was like the cosmos conspiring to help our family."

"And did the cosmos conspire to help you murder Adriana?"

Joe flinched. "Don't imagine for one moment that I'm happy about that. But I did what I had to do. I did it for my father and mother. Everything I do, I do for them."

"Including killing the hunter?"

"That was bad luck. He spotted me at the Balcony. I couldn't let him talk."

That was more than enough of a confession.

"Cosimo," I said. "Hold him off."

Joe's eyebrows shot up. Then surprise twisted into anger, and he took a step forward.

But Cosimo jumped in front of him, blocking him with fists raised. He bit down on his cigar. He punched the air a few times, as if warming up.

"Get out of my way, old man," Joe said, and tried to sweep Cosimo aside. But Cosimo landed a punch squarely in Joe's gut.

Joe staggered back, an affronted look on his face.

Meanwhile, I grabbed my phone and tapped "stop" on the audio recorder application. I saved the file. Then texted it to Chief Tedesco. A color bar showed the slow progress of transferring the file.

Joseph must've guessed what I was doing, because he ducked around Cosimo and dove toward his desk.

My phone made a satisfying whoosh sound.

I pushed back, rolling away on his chair, my hands raised.

"Done," I said, smiling. "Game over."

Joe sprawled across his desk, a desperate look on his face.

"No..."

The door opened.

"What is going on?" Mrs. Romano said. She glared at us, looking from me to Cosimo and then to her son. "Will someone tell me what this is about?"

Cosimo smiled around his cigar and sidled up to Mrs. Romano. "My dear lady," he said. "I'll explain. What's happening is this: this case is closed and you're paying my fee in full, plus expenses."

He glanced back at me. "*Our* fee."

34

The sounds of celebration within Moroni's followed me through the passage past Angelica's office and the bakery and down to the back door. I was carrying a bag of trash out. Angelica had closed the bakery for the day after it seemed that half of Carmine had turned up to celebrate.

They weren't celebrating me.

Well, Nat and Angelica and Chief Tedesco were. Even Cosimo had turned up, and was devouring his third tiramisu cup, while somehow keeping that soggy cigar in his mouth.

No, they were celebrating Lily. And so was I.

That morning, she got a letter from the culinary school. She got in. She would start next year. Her dream was coming true.

The old Bernie would've felt mixed emotions about it. Lily's dream was coming true, but what about me?

But I felt only happiness for Lily. She was doing what she was supposed to do—and so was I. Cosimo had officially offered me a steady job as his assistant investigator. A new chapter in my life was beginning.

I pushed open the back door and stepped out into the alleyway that ran behind the businesses on Garibaldi Avenue. I heaved the bag into the trash. And then froze.

Because I wasn't alone.

A man in a baseball cap and sunglasses stood in the alley.

"Bernie," he said.

"Bud."

"I wanted to thank you."

"All right."

"So," he said, scratching his beard. "Thank you."

Roberta appeared behind him. "There you are. We've got to get going. We've got a long way to go to your new hiding place. And we've got to get going before—"

"Before *they* find me?"

Bud stepped into the shadows under a metal staircase alongside the building, and he gazed up at the sky, as if expecting to see something. A helicopter, maybe. "Are they on to me?"

I looked from Bud to Roberta, and she gave me a little shake of the head. She said, "Don't worry, Bud. The Men in Black still have no clue where we're hiding you."

"Phew."

He tipped his baseball cap at me and walked away.

Roberta lingered for a moment.

"Is he—" I paused. "—all right?"

"He's got some crazy ideas," Roberta said. "But we wouldn't be protecting him if he didn't hold secrets that put his life at risk."

"What kind of secrets?"

"Bernie," Roberta said. "You know I can't tell you."

"Or you'd have to kill me?"

Her mouth twitched. Almost a smile. "Yes, something like that."

We said goodbye to each other, and I headed back inside to join the party.

When I walked into the bakery, Nat was leading the crowd in a full-throated rendition of "For She's a Jolly Good Fellow," which made Lily cover her face in embarrassment.

Chief Tedesco was leaning against the counter next to Angelica. I joined them.

"You did good, Bernie," Chief Tedesco said.

"Thanks."

"I agree," Cosimo said, joining us. "And I'm looking forward to you showing me how to install that antivirus software on my computer."

"You have a computer?"

He shrugged. "It's been sitting in my closet for a while. But I guess every self-respecting P.I. needs a computer these days."

Angelica said, "There's something else every self-respecting P.I. needs..." She crooked a finger, gesturing for me to follow her. "Come with me."

I followed her back outside to the alleyway.

She climbed the metal staircase. As far as I knew, it led to the upper story, which didn't contain anything—Angelica used it as an attic to store stuff.

I followed her. She unlocked the door and cracked it open.

We stepped into a wide-open space littered with boxes and old furniture. Dusty floorboards. Grimy windows overlooking Garibaldi Avenue.

Angelica led me into the middle, put an arm around my shoulders, and gestured at the space around us.

"You know what this is?"

I shook my head. "No, what is it?"

"An office."

I looked at her, my mouth dropping.

"P.I. Bernie Smyth's office," she said with a smile.

"Oh, Angelica."

I hugged her, and she squeezed me.

Then I let go and gazed around at the run-down space. My heart swelled. I could picture where my desk would go. And a couch. And filing cabinets.

It was perfect.

Above all, it was mine. Private Detective Bernie Smyth's very own private office.

THANK YOU for reading this Italian-American Cozy Mystery with Bernie and her friends.

Want a **free short story**? Sign up for my newsletter to hear when the next book comes out and I'll share the story with you:

https://mpblackbooks.com/newsletter/

If you enjoyed this book, please take a moment to **leave a review online**. It makes it easier for other readers to find the book. Thanks so much!

And while you wait for the next mystery with Bernie and her friends, turn the page for a preview of *The Art of Murder*, book 1 in the Parker Lee Mystery Series—a cozy featuring small-town journalist Parker Lee and her big, quirky family.

35

EXCERPT FROM THE ART OF
MURDER

My quirky Aunt Lil and I were standing on the back porch of her boutique hotel. We both leaned on the railing—me drinking coffee, she drinking nettle tea. Both of us admiring the view of the lake. It's not called Lakeview Inn for nothing.

"Who's that?"

Mist shrouded the little island half a mile out—Gull Island—and caught a figure in a rowboat. Then the person hauled on the oars with determination and escaped the fog. The prow cut a rippling line across the smooth lake as the boat headed toward the town docks.

"Whoever it is, he's out early," Aunt Lil said. "Or she—I can't tell."

The mug warmed my cold hands, and I took another sip. The thin hoodie I wore couldn't keep out the cool, morning air. I shivered a little. Aunt Lil, who wore her usual billowy muumuu, along with her talisman necklaces and jangly bangles, didn't seem fazed by the cold.

I said, "I'll need to leave for the symposium soon."

"And I want to spend some time clearing out more junk in the attic before the guests wake."

"Lots of guests?"

"Full house. The symposium's a hit."

I gave myself another 5 minutes. I took a deep breath. The air, cooled by the night, was as fresh as spring water. What could be better than early mornings in Allington? In the city, at this hour, there would be no rowboat gliding through an ethereal mist, only cars and trucks rumbling through smog.

The hinges on the door behind us creaked, then smacked shut, as someone stepped out onto the porch.

"There you are, Parker. Morning, Lil."

Mom joined us, leaning against the railing. In her police uniform, she contrasted sharply with her sister. In most things, she contrasted with her sister.

Aunt Lil said, "How's law and order, Charlie?"

"So far, so good."

"Well, I'll leave you two Lees alone. My attic needs some order."

Aunt Lil headed inside through the door that connected the porch to the inn's lounge. Even after the door closed, I could hear the jangling of her bangles.

Mom's uniform was, as always, neatly pressed. On her chest, the badge that said "Chief" shone. So did the brass name tag with "C. Lee" engraved. Both spotless.

She looked out at the lake.

"Who's out there?"

"I was wondering about that," I said.

"Strange to be rowing back from the island this early."

"Maybe it's a fisherman."

In that instant, the rowboat vanished, slipping behind the town's main docks and out of sight.

I took another sip of coffee. The sun made an appearance. Across Allington Cove, on the opposite headland of our little cove, a big Victorian mansion, like the Lakeview Inn, glowed in the light. Broadstairs House. My childhood home. Which I'd returned to after leaving the city.

I'd dreamed of a successful career in journalism in the city, and it hadn't worked out. After coming back home, I'd felt ashamed. But I fallen in love with Allington all over again. It was where I belonged.

Although sometimes I still missed the action—the sensational stories—of the big city.

I forced my attention from the lake to my little town—and up Chestnut Hill to Larke House. The symposium would be starting soon. On the lake, the mist was growing thinner as the sun rose higher over the woods.

"Strange," Mom repeated, still staring toward the docks. "What was he doing out there?"

"Probably nothing news worthy," I said.

Mom glanced at me.

"You've got somewhere to be this morning. Otherwise you wouldn't sound so dismissive."

"Dad wants me to cover the symposium at Larke House."

"Of course. A couple of hundred art historians convening to discuss Julia Larke's life and legacy."

"You sound like the symposium program."

I dug up the rolled-up program out of the back pocket of my jeans and waved it at her to show I was already up to speed.

"Miranda gave me tons of reading material," I said. "She sure makes Larke sound important. But then that's her job, right—to make Julia Larke sound important?"

"Larke is important," Mom corrected me. "Here in Allington we've always known her artwork was special.

Imagine if she finally gets the worldwide recognition she deserves. That's a big deal." Then she smiled. "Besides, it's Joy's favorite artist."

My older sister Joy owned Cafe Larke, Allington's coziest coffee house. Larke's artwork decorated the walls of the cafe as well as Joy's bedroom at Broadstairs House. And she could recite an endless ream of facts about the artist's life. Even before Miranda, the director of Larke House, gave me a heap of reading material, I'd heard a lot about Julia Larke. But I'd never been especially interested.

I swirled the coffee in my cup. Almost empty. Almost time to go.

Mom said, "You're dragging your feet. Don't you want to do this assignment?"

"I thought Dad was doing it."

Mom said nothing. Forget about the gun she carried—silence was her most powerful weapon.

I sighed. "No, I don't want to do it. The news story about the symposium will be dry, boring stuff. Paint-by-numbers journalism."

"Not like the stories you covered in the big city."

"I didn't say that."

Mom said no more. She was staring at me with that familiar stony-faced look. The silent interrogation. Waiting for the person in the hot seat to break down and blab. I could pretend not to notice, but Chief of Police Lee could play this game until the sun set, and I had an assignment today.

"All right," I said with a sigh. "The stories aren't like the ones I covered in the big city."

"Every story in *The Gazette* can't be about fraud or murder."

"That's what Dad told me. 'A news article about a

murder can be ten times as boring as one about a lost kitten. It's all about how you tell the story.'"

"Your dad's a wise man," Mom said.

"And you're a little biased."

"Forty years of bias." She smiled. "But I can objectively say your dad knows what he's talking about."

She was right, of course. Dad ran *The Allington Gazette*, the local newspaper, carrying on a tradition that stretched back generations. If anyone knew about local news reporting, it was my dad.

I drained the dregs from my coffee cup. "Dad's right. It's all about how you tell the story. And that's why I'm going to get to Larke House early and give this story a decent shot. Like you said, it's a big deal that Julia Larke is finally getting the recognition she deserves."

I lifted my messenger bag off the deck and slung it over my shoulder.

Mom put a hand on my arm, stopping me.

"Park," she said. "I'm glad you're back."

"I'm glad I'm back, too."

"I just want you to know that I'm aware it hasn't been easy. I know Allington isn't as exciting as—"

Something crashed above us, and I jumped.

I looked up, and so did Mom.

A window flew open under the eaves of the roof.

"Charlie," Aunt Lil yelled. "I could use some of that law and order up here—and I'm not talking about organizing boxes."

Want more? Grab *The Art of Murder* at your favorite online bookstore.

MORE BY M.P. BLACK

A Wonderland Books Cozy Mystery Series

A Bookshop to Die For

A Theater to Die For

A Halloween to Die For

A Christmas to Die For

A Yarn Shop to Die For

A Hair Salon to Die For

An Italian-American Cozy Mystery Series

The Soggy Cannoli Murder

Sambuca, Secrets, and Murder

Tastes Like Murder

Meatballs, Mafia, and Murder

Tiramisu or Murder

Parker Lee Mystery Series

The Art of Murder

The Deadly Circle

Trouble Brewing

A Killer View

Short stories

The Italian Cream Cake Murder (FREE)

ABOUT THE AUTHOR

M.P. Black writes fun cozies with an emphasis on food, books, and travel—and, of course, a good old murder mystery.

Besides writing and publishing his own books, he helps others fulfill their author dreams too through courses and coaching.

M.P. Black has lived in many places, including Brooklyn, Vienna, and San Jose de Costa Rica. Today, he and his family live in Copenhagen, Denmark, where coziness ("hygge") is a national pastime.

Join M.P. Black's free newsletter to download a free story and get updates on books and special deals:

https://mpblackbooks.com/newsletter/